The Love
Magnet
of
Oz

Also by Alan Lindsay
> *The Burzee Rose*
> *Stolen to Oz*
> *A. a novel*
> *Ambaguam, Beginning at the End*

With Dennis Anfuso
> *OzHouse*
> *OzHouse Reopened, The Curse of Budistiltskin*

The
Love
Magnet of
Oz

Interset Press

2022

9 8 7 6 5 4 3 2 1 /0 1

Interset Press

35 Burns Hill Road

Wilton, New Hampshire 03086

Interset Press is a registered trademark and "Fiddler," the Interset Press colophon, is a trademark of Linda Anfuso.

Printed in the United States of America.

First Interset Press edition: June 2022.

Library of Congress Cataloguing-in-Publication Data:

Lindsay, Alan

Title: **The Love Magnet of Oz**

Summary: There's a new witch in the broken castle of the Wicked Witch of the West. She calls herself The Sorceress Lady Mumps. She wants to make all of Oz her own. All she needs is three clever cronies and a powerful weapon. Meanwhile, at Reed Elementary, Mildred finds an old magnet stuck to the buckle of her old boot. Louise recognizes it immediately. But this charm has more magic than anyone ever knew. When Mildred and Louise and their friend Thaddeus and their enemy Sam find themselves at odds with Mumps in Oz, they realize just how powerful the magnet is.

[1. Fantasy. 2. Oz. 3. Lindsay, Alan.] 1. Title [Fic.]

Paperback ISBN: 978-1-57433-050-2

Illustrations and cover art by Dennis Anfuso

Book design by Guy Ravin

For
Motto and Bot

One

Mildred was trying to look like she had some place to be. Eyes front, head down, she tramped across the playground in the clunky boots her mother made her wear because it was supposed to be muddy today (but it wasn't). She moved in a straight line from the door of the sixth-grade wing to the jungle gym. She didn't like the jungle gym—pulling yourself up on the cold metal just to get to the top so you could lower yourself back down again. What was the point? And she was wearing a dress, which her mother told her she had to, and she wasn't supposed to climb on the jungle gym in a dress. She preferred the swings or the teeter-totter, but it was very hard to get a swing, and you needed a partner for the teeter-totter.

Over by the door, the popular kids were playing kickball. She wanted to play kickball. But no one ever asked her to, not since that one time (it was her first day at Edgerton Elementary) when she was picked for a team, and she kicked the soft rubber ball with all her might. It made a thwangy sound and the pitcher scooped it up and chased her to the base and threw it at her.

He missed.

She knew he missed. Even though he was very close and it was an easy out, and he didn't usually miss even when he threw from far away. But he *did* miss. She never felt even a shadow of a touch of the ball on her back. But he yelled: "out." And Mildred landed on the base and stood there. "I got you," he said. "I got you. You're out."

"No. No, you didn't."

"You saw, I got her." He looked around. Every face was blank. "I got her," he said again. And that brought them around.

"He got you," they said. His name was Donny. Everyone wanted to be in his gang of cool kids.

"No, he didn't," Mildred said. "It never touched me." And she stood on the base. But even her own team said, "Mildred, he got you. You're out."

"But he didn't get me. He didn't. He missed me. I'm safe."

She stood on first base, pleading her case. But Samantha, a girl she didn't have any reason to hate yet, walked over and stared down at her and said, "You're out. Get off the stupid base."

"But he missed me."

And then Samantha pushed her off the base, pushed her hard enough to knock her down, but she didn't actually fall. She reached her foot back to the base. Samantha pushed her again, harder, and this time she did fall. Right on her butt. But she was right, so she did what her mother always told her she should do: she stood her ground (even though she was actually lying in the dirt); she stretched her foot back to the base.

Samantha grabbed the ball and
threw it at her as hard as she could.
Mildred could smell the rubber and feel
the coolness kind of form itself around
her head like a pillow or like clay
squished around a rock. But it was soft
in a way, even though it pushed her
head back and, worse than that, pushed
her glasses into her nose till it hurt. But
that only took a second before the ball
bounced back and flew all the way to the
shortstop in the air. And Samantha said,

"There. Now you're out. Get off the stupid base." Samantha wasn't
very good with words.

No one picked Mildred to play again after that.

Even though she was safe.

Mildred walked around the jungle gym grabbing the cold metal
and letting it slip through her hand. It felt like it was wet, but it was
dry.

On the other side of the playground, it was Samantha's turn to
kick the ball. Donny bowled it in toward her and Samantha ran up
to it and put a charge into it. Samantha was the biggest jerk in the
school. Mildred told her mother if she was a boy she'd say she was
a bully.

"Can't a girl be a bully?" her mother replied.

Mildred didn't know. She'd always thought only boys were
bullies.

The ball sailed over the kickball field and headed toward the hill
where the monkey bars were. It didn't hit the ground until Samantha

was already at first base. Justin chased after the ball, which bounced near the bottom of the hill and kept going up right into the monkey bars, like skee-ball in one of those cups. Samantha was heading to second base. She was going to get a home run.

Mildred wanted to get her out. She reached into the monkey bars. Justin said, "Don't touch it." But Mildred grabbed it and tossed it to Justin so he could get Samantha out.

"Fan interference," Donny yelled. "Fan interference, doesn't count."

"What," Samantha snarled, and she stared over at Mildred with eyes like lasers, and she showed her teeth.

"Do over," Donny said.

And Samantha was still glaring at Mildred, which made her nervous but also made her want to stick her tongue out. Samantha had to kick it again. And Justin was way back near the monkey bars when she did. Donny rolled the ball in, and Samantha put another charge into it. It went even higher than the first time—waaaaaay up. And that gave Justin more time to get a bead on it. Which he did.

It came down like a baby in his arms.

"You're out," Donny yelled.

And Mildred chuckled.

Samantha fumed.

At the back of the classroom when the teacher went into the hallway to talk to another teacher, Samantha said, "What kind of name is Mildred? *MIL*-dred? Who names their kid *MILLLL*-dred?"

When Samantha said that, Mildred felt like about a million bugs started moving around inside her stomach. She was in the middle of drawing a picture of a turtle. At first she didn't say anything. But then Samantha asked the question again, "Huh? Huh? What kind of a name is MIL-DRED?"

"It's my grandmother's name," Mildred said. She stood her ground.

"Oh, it's her grandmother's name."

Some of the kids laughed, but in a slow uncomfortable way. Most of the kids didn't make any sound at all. Mildred did not look up. She kept drawing.

Samantha said, "She must be pretty ugly if they called her MIL-dred. Sounds like mildew. Grandma Mildew."

Mildred still didn't look up. She spoke quietly as if there were no bugs in her stomach trying to find a way out. "It was a very common name when my grandmother was a girl."

"Well it's a stupid name now." Samantha put her face right down next to Mildred's desk. Mildred wanted to poke her in the eye with her pencil. But she didn't. She just kept drawing and said nothing for as long as she could.

Mildred's mother knew everything there was to know about bullies. She was a child psychologist. And when Mildred told her about Samantha, her mother sat her down and explained a few things, and then she pretended to be Samantha and showed her the kinds of things that Samantha was going to say and do if she was really a bully. And when her mother was the pretend Samantha and Mildred was pretending to be herself, Mildred said, "Someone with a watermelon on her face shouldn't make fun of other people's noses." But her mother said that would only get her hit.

Samantha snarled across Mildred's desk.

"Old names are becoming popular again," Mildred said.

Her mother said it was a good idea to stay calm and pretend she wasn't being bullied. But she hadn't mentioned that there would be bugs in her stomach. "Make sure you stand your ground," her mother had said. "Bullies hate that. It's all about the easy victory for a bully. They're basically cowards."

Mildred had to pee.

"Your name is as ugly as you are," said Samantha.

Mildred put spots on the legs of the turtle and gave it a tail.

"Artists don't need to be beautiful," said Mildred. She was feeling like the bugs inside her were growing like crazy and moving out of her stomach and down her legs and up her arms, but she hoped Samantha couldn't tell.

"Leave her alone," said Justin.

"Shut up, Justin," said Samantha. And Justin shut up.

"Oh, so you're an artist. Let me see." And she grabbed the picture from Mildred's hands. "That's the worst turtle I've ever seen. What even is this? Is it supposed to be some kind of animal? My cat could draw a better—a better thing."

Mildred blurted, "You just," but then she stopped. She wanted to point out that a person can't pretend they don't know what something is after they've already called it what it is. But she didn't say that. Her mother told her how to deal with Samantha and it was just the opposite of what she wanted to do.

"I just what?" Samantha asked.

Mildred breathed. "That's why I'm practicing," she said, pronouncing every syllable carefully. And she didn't ask for her drawing back. She just took out another piece of paper.

"Well you are going to have to practice for a million years because you're hopeless. You'll never be able to be an artist. You couldn't draw a stick."

"Practice makes perfect," said Mildred, as calmly as she could.

She drew a stick. She added a little leaf at the top.

At home that evening, she video chatted with Louise and Thaddeus. They were her best friends from her old school, Reed Elementary. They'd got together because they all had what their teacher had called old-fashioned names. "The thing is," Mildred said, "there's a girl who started school two weeks *after* me and she already has *three* friends. And I don't have any."

"You had plenty of friends here," said Louise.

"She already has *three*," Mildred repeated.

"Is she pretty?" said Thaddeus.

"What difference does that make?" said Louise.

"Of course it makes a difference," said Thaddeus. "Do you know any pretty girl that doesn't have as many friends as she wants to?"

"That's not fair," said Louise.

"What's 'fair' got to do with it?" said Thaddeus.

"No," Mildred said at last. "She's not especially pretty. She's just ordinary like me."

"Well, you know you don't have the personality to just make friends, Mildred," Louise said.

"You're too stubborn and you don't go up to talk to people," Thaddeus said.

"I'm not stubborn. I'm just right more often than other people."

"Who do you sit with at lunch?" Louise said.

"I eat by myself. I wolf it down, and then I go to the monkey bars."

"You hate the monkey bars," Thaddeus said.

"You should find some people to sit with," Louise said.

"Do you want me to walk up to a group of people and push myself on them?"

"Just say, 'can I sit with you?'" Thaddeus said.

"Yeah, and then they give you the hairy eyeball and don't say anything. And then they ignore you when you sit there anyway, and you feel stupid."

"Mildred, they'll like you if they get to know you," Thaddeus said.

"I tried that. I sucked at kickball."

"What about the Love Magnet?" Louise said.

"That doesn't work, obviously," Mildred said. She reached into her pocket and pulled out a scarred and rusty horseshoe magnet and turned it around.

"Of course it doesn't work. It's a toy," Thaddeus said.

"How do you know?"

"It hasn't worked yet. Thaddeus is right."

"It's from a story," Thaddeus said. "Even if magic was real, which it isn't, that's just a story someone made up."

"How do you know it isn't real?" Louise asked.

"Because science," said Thaddeus.

"It's a toy," said Mildred. "It's not the real Love Magnet." And that stopped the conversation between Louise and Thaddeus from boiling over without Mildred having to decide whether magic was real or not.

The magnet or toy was the size of her hand. It wasn't the real Love Magnet, but it was a real magnet. It had once been red with white tips. The words "A Love Magnet" were etched lightly into its surface, the *A* on the left side, *Love* at the bottom and *Magnet* on the right. It was old and had been painted more than once. It was the age and the scratches that made Louise think it might be real. Mildred played along because she knew when they found it she was going to a new school soon and a Love Magnet might come in handy.

Plus, the way she found it, it made it seem like she was supposed to have it, like it was looking for her. She and Louise and Thaddeus were taking the back way home from Reed Elementary on a mild winter day. They could have taken the bus. But they didn't live all that far away, and they didn't mind walking home on nice days. Besides, walking home was faster than the bus because the bus had to go all the way around on the roads, but they could take a shortcut through the trees. Plus, they took second bus, which meant it first had to go all the way up the road in the wrong direction and empty out all the kids and then come back and pick up the second batch. But if you cut through a short path behind the school you came out right in the neighborhood where Thaddeus lived. And if you followed the road past his house and crossed Bedford Road, you came to the neighborhood where Mildred and Louise lived. And if you took a certain path through the woods where the kids rode their minibikes and snowmobiles, you could make it home before second bus even got back to school to pick the second kids up.

At Reed Elementary, the shortcut went through a tear in the fence, and you had to cross right by a driveway where a loud but harmless dog lived. That was where the magnet found Mildred. She was wearing her big boots that had been her mother's boots when she was a girl (her mother wasn't the kind of person to throw perfectly good things away even if everyone said they were funky) because there was snow on the ground, and the boots had metal buckles. And when she stopped to wait for Thaddeus to push aside the fence so he could climb through, she felt a tug on her foot. And there, clinging to her boot, was the magnet.

"What the…" Mildred had said.

Louise stooped down to pick it up. She recognized it immediately. Not many kids these days would have any idea what it was. But Louise loved to read even more than Mildred did, and she'd read absolutely everything, including all the books in the *Wizard of Oz* series. And there was one called *The Road to Oz* in which the Love Magnet appeared.

"But it's just like the one from the book," Louise said to Thaddeus and Mildred in the video chat.

"But the one in the book is brown," Mildred said.

"Except for that," Louise said. "Somebody must have painted it."

"It's just merchandizing from like a hundred years ago that probably the old guy who lives in the house with the dog lost," Thaddeus said. He had never believed in the magnet, not even in fun.

"I know," Mildred said.

"Well then why do you carry it?" Louise asked. "Why does she carry it?" she repeated to Thaddeus.

"My mother said that if you believe something is lucky then you expect to have good luck, and that makes you look for luck, and that makes you find luck, and so there you have it. It's a self-filling thingything."

"But you're not having any luck," Thaddeus said.

"Yet," Louise shot back.

Mildred did not like Edgerton Elementary at all. Samantha harassed her most days even though she never got a rise out of her (so her mother wasn't exactly right about that), and she didn't have any friends to support her. Justin seemed like he might want to be her friend. But Justin was clearly afraid of Samantha and wasn't willing to take the chance of making a friend out of the kid no one liked. She would have found it impossible to handle except that Reed Elementary wasn't far away at all, and Thaddeus and Louise had no trouble getting their parents to drive them to Mildred's house on the weekends.

It was a cold, damp day. The air was heavy and thick. Not an ideal day to go outside. Still, Mildred brought Louise and Thaddeus to her new school so they could use the swings and the teeter-totter.

They did not expect to find Samantha there.

"Just ignore her," Louise said.

"You didn't say you've got the coolest playground," Thaddeus said.

It was true, Edgerton Elementary had about twice as many things to climb on, slide down, pull yourself up in or run around than Reed Elementary did. And most of it was new. Louise ran to the newest thing of all, which they called "Castle Park." It had monkey bars and rings and a climbing wall and two slides (one of which was a tube) and made a kind of fort area underneath and on top.

But Mildred didn't want to play. She wanted to hide. She wanted to wait for Samantha to go away.

"What's she doing here, anyway, on a Saturday?" Louise joined Thaddeus and Mildred in the fort under Castle Park.

"Same thing we're doing," Thaddeus said.

Louise said, "Do we really have to hide in here?" She peeked through one of the foot holes in the climbing wall. Samantha was on the other side of the parking lot. She hadn't noticed them. She made no move to come over or go away. She was standing on the circle where the busses dropped you off as though she were waiting for someone.

"Her mother works here," Mildred said. "She's a teacher in one of the lower grades."

Samantha kicked a rock, and then looked over as though she'd heard something. She looked twice. Thaddeus held his breath. Mildred rolled her eyes. Samantha started walking over. Samantha was bad enough when there was a teacher just outside the door. Now, there was no one around. Who knew what she was capable of?

"But there's three of us," Louise said.

"I don't think that's going to bother her," Mildred said.

"Who's under there?"

Nobody spoke. Samantha was still a ways away.

"This is stupid," Louise whispered.

"Don't you know you're not allowed on the playground on Saturday? School property," Samantha yelled, still coming forward.

"Give me the Love Magnet," Louise said.

"What for?" Thaddeus said.

"Because…" Louise said.

"Like she doesn't have enough to make fun of? You're gonna charge out there and point a toy magnet at her like it was a light saber or something?"

But Louise happened to know that the Love Magnet was in the pocket of Mildred's jacket.

Samantha climbed up the hill.

"Mildew, is that you in there?"

Louise reached into Mildred's jacket and grabbed the magnet and handed it to Mildred. "Use it," she said as she put it in Mildred's hand.

Samantha put her hands on the bar above her head and leaned in, smirking like something out of a cartoon. Louise grabbed Mildred's hand and aimed the magnet right at her.

Samantha chuckled. "What the…what is that?"

Mildred's hand began to shake. The magnet twitched between her fingers, and then it pulled—hard. It felt like it was going to fly out of her hands. But not at Samantha. It was going to fly out of her hands into the metal crossbar Samantha's hands were holding onto, just above the smugness of her eyes. Mildred put two hands on the magnet, but it pulled so hard, it made her stand up. Thaddeus grabbed her left arm. Louise held on to her right. And all three together were thrown into the crossbar. It was like someone had almost picked them right off the ground like little stones. They were thrown with so much force they piled into Samantha like she was carrying a football and they were tackling her. In a moment all four of them were on the ground in a heap.

"Hey," Samantha yelled, "What the…. Get off of me you…"

The three stunned friends gathered their wits and pushed and rolled and kicked their way off Samantha. But even in their frenzy they couldn't help but notice how everything had changed. The day had turned warm and bright, and the smell of dirt had changed into the smell of grass. In a  moment Mildred was kneeling and Thaddeus, who had landed flat on his stomach, was pulling his knees toward his chest to pick himself up. Louise was sitting on the ground like a balled-up sheet of paper. They all paused. Samantha pulled herself up onto her elbows and squinted. The air smelled faintly of smoke, and overhead a cantankerous flock of birds was passing like a swift black cloud.

Two

The stories out of the Winkie country left Ozma befuddled. Just a little. Or perhaps little more than a little.

Befuddled.

That was the perfect word. It was obvious from the way she leaned forward on her Emerald Throne and rolled her scepter across her lap as though it were a rolling pin and her thighs were dough.

"Really?" she said. And she lowered her eyes and moved her head back and forth as though she were following the path of a mouse looping across the floor. "Smoke?" she said.

"I've seen it with my own eyes," said the Winkie ambassador. "Someone must have moved into the abandoned castle of the Wicked Witch. For many days, great clouds of smoke have been rising from the top of the high hill, sometimes green, sometimes orange, sometimes black."

"Why would anyone do that?" Ozma asked the Winkie, whose name was Sakem.

"Well, it can't be anyone with good intentions." Sakem had been one of the slaves of the Wicked Witch many years ago. She'd been plucked one day from her farm by the strong and stealthy arms of a winged monkey and flown to that very castle when it was at the height of its horrible power, and she'd been forced to serve the Wicked Witch until the day that the noble Dorothy had melted her and freed all the slaves. Ever since, she'd kept a distant, watchful eye on the place as the woods slowly rose around it and the wooden roofs of the stone castle began to fall. She was the first one to warn the Tin Woodman, the Emperor of the Winkies, of the new threat. No one had yet dared to go look for themselves.

The castle had been uninhabited for many years. No one—as far as anyone knew—had ventured near it since Dorothy had thrown the bucket of water on the dusty old witch and she and Toto and the Cowardly Lion had escaped so easily under the protection of the very Winkies who had, as slaves of the witch, imprisoned her. There might as well have been an invisible fence that ran about half a mile distant around the base of the hollowed-out granite mountain on which the crumbling castle stood. In the old days, the days of the standoff between the Witch and the Wizard, there had been no trees for a great distance around the castle. The one-eyed witch had cut them all down so that no one could sneak up on her. And if anyone came near her domain, the lonely witch had wolves and crows and bees and Winkie slaves (and even, for a while, the winged monkeys) whom she could send out to capture them to make them slaves or tear them to pieces, so that whether the intruders were there to attack her or whether they had just strayed within her sight, her enemies always made her stronger.

But that was a time so long ago no one ever thought about it anymore. Since then a forest had taken root and, although the castle was still visible from afar, for more than 100 years the w oods had expanded through the cleared fields so that no one in the castle's vicinity could know that that was where they were unless they wandered into the very inner ring at the base of the solitary mountain, where nothing but a few hardy grasses struggled for life, the ground there was so dry.

The only thing Sakem knew for sure was that there were fires burning in the ruins and that a large flock of birds had taken up residence there. They did not seem to be wild birds. Or if they were,

they were a very well-choreographed flock of wild birds. Every morning they flew out from the castle in extraordinary numbers, appearing at first to be a huge cloud of smoke. Then they bobbed over the sky in a black wave until they came to the side of the forest that bordered the farmland of the Winkies, where they circled in an ever-changing shape that was sometimes like a ball and sometimes like a net and sometimes like the surface of an ocean. All the while they spread out and came together in their changing shapes. By itself this would have been merely fun to watch, but all the while they tweeted and twittered in a horrid screech of disjointed notes that reminded everyone of stories they'd read of threatening and ominous volumes of acres of cicadas just before they stripped the fields bare. And then, as though someone had whistled for them, the whole flock all at once flew back to the castle as though they were a single bird. During their whole flight out and back, they did not land and they did not talk, not in words. At least no one had heard them say anything. But the noise they made still sounded like a threat, like someone sent to tell the people to lay down their weapons when the soldiers came through so no one would get hurt.

"If we could put those sounds into the sounds of our words," Sakem said, "I think that is exactly what they would say." The Winkies were growing restless and scared.

No one in Oz had ever seen this type of bird before. They were very small, each all one color, some blue and some white and some black. They did not have feet.

"Of course they must have feet," Ozma said. "They must just be too small to see."

"As you wish," Sakem said.

The little birds (they were really quite small) flew over the fields and vast farmlands of the Land of the Winkies farther into the territory every day, always as though they were looking for something.

"Have they caused trouble?" asked the princess.

"Not yet," said Sakem. "But did I mention the horrible noise of their constant tweeting and twittering, scaring the animals and the people too? And did I say how dark it gets under the cloud of birds and how cold? And there seem to be more and more of them every day. And the smell of the smoke? We're afraid they will come for our corn and our wheat like locusts and starve us."

The girl princess rolled her scepter back and forth over her thighs. "What kind of bird do you suppose they are?"

"Does that matter?" asked Sakem.

"Yes, very much. If they are bug-eating birds, then you have nothing to fear from them—except for the noise, and that is something you could get used to in time, perhaps, if it comes and goes like the rain, that is. Rain is something that keeps us inside when we'd rather go out and play. But if we wait it out, it moves on and the sunshine returns. Perhaps these birds are like that."

"How very wise," Sakem said. "It is no mere chance that you are the Princess of Oz with wisdom like that."

"Besides," Ozma said, ignoring the praise, since praise made it harder to think, "besides, rain we know is good for the earth even if it keeps us indoors. It feeds the plants and helps make food for us all. Perhaps these birds too will eat the bugs that attack the plants and improve the crop and make farming easier and more pleasant. And so we will more easily put up with the unpleasant sound of the tweets and the twitters and even grow to like them knowing what good the tweeters do."

"And this is why our excellent-hearted emperor has sent me to you, to learn your wisdom before attempting to solve the problem himself."

But the next time the Winkie messenger returned to the Emerald City, Ozma did not receive the good news she was hoping for.

"The birds do not eat insects," said Sakem.

"What do they eat?" asked the princess. "Not corn I hope."

"Not corn, my princess."

"Phew!" said Ozma.

"Not 'phew' either," said Sakem.

"Not 'phew'?" said Ozma.

"Worms," said Sakem.

"Well, phew," Ozma insisted. "I was afraid they were dangerous. What good are worms?"

"Not 'phew' at all," said Sakem. "We need worms."

"You need worms?" Ozma screwed up her face.

"A few."

"A few?"

"A lot, actually," said Sakem. "Every lot needs a lot of worms."

"Now I am confused," said Ozma.

"Worms fertilize the soil and keep it light and open for the rain to get in. Worms make roots healthy and keep water running to the corn. We definitely need worms."

Ozma wondered if there might be some way to do what worms do without worms.

"But it's worse than that," said the messenger. "To get the worms, these birds dig with their claws and their beaks, which are strong and fierce as an eagle's, although they themselves are small. And if the worm is hiding in the corn roots, the birds rips out the corn to get at the worm. And so even though they will not eat the corn, they destroy a lot of corn."

"I thought you said they didn't have feet," said Ozma.

Sakem paused to remember. "I did, didn't I." She paused again in thought. "Oh, but they do have feet, all right. And now that I think of it, it seems as though they've been put together a piece at a time. Oh, I should have expected that birds living in the bowels of the castle of the Wicked Witch would not be a help to the Land of Oz. I also think they are getting bigger."

Sakem suggested that Ozma use the magic picture.

"Tried that already," said the princess. "The first time I asked, it showed me a great cloud of birds. The second time I asked it showed me a large woman in a pink gown standing on the battlements of a castle with the birds swirling around her. The third time I asked, it showed me nothing at all."

"Nothing at all?"

"Just a blank picture. It seems to be broken."

So there was nothing to do but to send a party of faithful envoys to the ruins to find out what all the smoke and birds were all about. And so the princess requested that the honorable Scarecrow of Oz, who was visiting the Emerald City at the time, accompany Sakem back to the land of the Winkies. Surely if anyone knew how to scare birds away from corn it would be the Scarecrow. And so, mounting the back of the Cowardly Lion, the trusty Scarecrow made his way to the Emperor of the Winkies with all the haste he could muster.

The next time Sakem returned to the Emerald City, the news was even worse. The Scarecrow, the Tin Woodman and the Cowardly Lion had gone together to find out what these birds were up to and who had dared to cross the forest and re-inhabit the ruin of the castle of the Wicked Witch of the West. But they had not returned, nor had they sent back any messenger to tell of their progress. And the birds were still coming daily to kill the corn. And they were definitely getting bigger.

"The Shaggy Man saw the Scarecrow and the Cowardly Lion and the Tin Woodman, for he lives in a little hut between the Winkie capital and the castle. So we know they made it that far. They have had more than time enough to travel from his hut to the castle and back."

So the great princess called another band of her loyal subjects to her throne, Scraps, the Patchwork Girl; Tik-Tok, the mechanical man, and Professor H. M. Wogglebug, T. E., and she sent them to find the Tin Woodman, the Scarecrow, and the Cowardly Lion, and to find out what was going on in the old castle.

Three

There was no playground anywhere. "How do you lose a playground when you're in it?" Thaddeus wanted to know.

"I lost the magnet," Mildred said as though she were answering his question.

"But that's the Love Magnet," Louise said. "We can't lose it." But rather than fall on the ground to grope around for it, she told Thaddeus to help Mildred look for it. Louise was busy trying to understand what had happened and where they were. She turned her head on every side with a quizzical look on her face. "Really?" she said to herself. "Is it really…?" Unsatisfied with what she could see, she raised herself to her tip toes, as though doing so might help her to see farther over the wide field, and then, when that didn't work, she did two or three two-footed, twisting hops, taking in various points of the compass.

In the direction of the sun everything was a field of yellow-brown grass. There were sunflowers and buttercups growing wild. On the north and west sides stood dark woods full of birch with yellow leaves as though it were fall—which should mean they were somewhere in the southern hemisphere since it was spring when they were on the playground. But the sun seemed too high and bright for fall, and the weather was too warm.

"What are you doing, ballet?" Samantha sneered. Samantha was staring at her with her hands on her hips. Louise ignored her.

Toward the south, just on the horizon, silos stood out against the sky.

"It's not here," said Mildred.

"We have bigger problems than a lost toy," said Thaddeus.

"That's true. But it's not a toy. It's the Love Magnet. People don't always like strangers," said Louise.

"No, no, I mean, what just happened? And how do we get back home?" Thaddeus took out his phone.

"It pulled us here," Mildred said. "Louise is right. It's obviously not a toy. We need it to get home."

"Oh," said Louise. "I didn't think of that."

"No service, no internet," said Thaddeus. Everyone took out their phones.

"That's impossible," said Mildred.

Louise waved to Samantha to join Mildred and Thaddeus on the ground as she herself got down on her knees. Mildred drew a circle around where they landed, so they would know where to look.

"What are you talking about?" Samantha tramped up to the friends and stared down at them. She looked slightly mountainous from that angle.

"The magnet," Mildred said slowly. "We need to find it to get back home." She combed the tall grasses with her hands.

"I don't think it brought us here," said Thaddeus.

"But it did. It pulled us. You felt it. We need it to get home," Mildred said.

"But it's just a magnet. That's not what they do," Thaddeus said. "And where even are we?"

"We're in the Winkie country," Louise rose up to her knees. She'd been waiting for someone to ask. Then she stood up and pointed across the field, eastward, she believed. "And you can bet the emperor's tin castle is over there somewhere. And, who knows, maybe Dorothy herself, and the Lion and everyone, maybe they came by right by here when they killed the Wicked Witch of the West."

Samantha took her arms off her hips and folded them in front of her chest, then she curled her lip into her mouth and made a face that looked puzzled and mean at the same time. "You don't have any idea where we are."

"I know exactly where we are," said Louise, turning her head toward her.

"Where do you *think* we are?" Samantha asked.

"Like I just said, we're in the Winkie Country of the Land of Oz."

"We'll never find it in this grass," said Thaddeus. "If only we had another magnet, or a piece of steel." He felt his pockets to see if he'd brought his Swiss Army knife.

"Yeah, right," Samantha scoffed.

"Everything's yellow," said Louise. "Look. All yellow flowers."

"Listen, stupid, I'm not dumb enough to think we're in a book."

"We're not in a book. We're in Oz. They wrote books about it," said Louise. "You do know the difference, don't you?"

Samantha stared hard at Louise. Louise, although she was much shorter than Samantha, stared right back.

Mildred glanced up, then looked away. She pretended to be looking for the magnet but she was really watching Samantha out of the corner of her eye in case she tried to hurt Louise.

Mildred said, as though to no one, "Four people will be able to find their way home easier than three."

Louise looked straight at Samantha: "Now help us find the magnet, Samantha." Then she lowered herself back to the ground.

Samantha just stood there. Mildred glanced up. She looked past Samantha as though she was curious about something behind her, but really she was looking at Samantha. Samantha sneered down at her. If she had to guess, Mildred would have said Samantha was trying to figure out which one of them she was going to kick first.

"If a car has three wheels that work and one that doesn't, it won't get anywhere," said Mildred.

"Where do you come up with this crap?" Samantha spat.

"That's all I'm saying," said Mildred.

Samantha didn't move or speak. She pulled her neck back and made a face like she'd just bit into a big hunk of baking chocolate she'd thought was a candy bar.

"Are you going to help or not?" Louise asked.

"Louise," Mildred pleaded.

"You want me to crawl around on the ground like a baby looking for a toy?"

Mildred said: "If we don't find the magnet we might be stuck here forever."

"Where the freak are we?" Samantha repeated as though to herself. "And how did we get here?"

"Wow. You must've hit your head pretty hard," said Thaddeus.

"Shut up, turkey face."

Thaddeus shut up.

"We've already explained where we are *and* how we got here," said Mildred.

"Now help us find the magnet or go away," said Louise.

"What did you say?" Samantha stared hard at Louise.

"Look, either you're going to help us or we don't need to help you." Louise looked hard at Samantha then turned away—as though she were looking at something on the southern horizon she hadn't noticed before. She was letting Samantha know she wasn't afraid. Samantha came up behind her in three strides and pushed her hard on the back. Louise stumbled forward and fell on her face on the ground.

"Whoever asked you to help me, dumb ass?"

Thaddeus watched, frozen. Mildred rose to her knees and yelled out. Louise didn't move or speak. Samantha's long shadow was laid out beside her on the ground.

"You *are* a bully," Mildred said.

"What of it?" said Samantha. "You're a stupid bunch of losers."

"Really?" said Louise. "Did you spend all day coming up with that one? 'Stupid bunch of losers'?" She looked directly at Samantha. "What do you think, Mildred, should someone with such a genius vocabulary be calling anyone stupid?"

"Actually, she can be pretty good with insults," said Mildred.

The weird compliment slowed Sam down a moment. She didn't know whether to say "thank you" or "hey!"

But then Louise said, "Maybe it's Oz then. What do you think, Sammy. Oz making you stupid?"

Mildred was pretty sure her mother would say that that was not the best technique for dealing with bullies. Louise turned away and ran her fingers slowly through the grass.

Samantha's shadow raised its foot and arms as high as they would go, like the shadow of a stomping giant. Mildred called out. Louise rolled out of the way just as the heavy foot came down and pounded the grass where her back would have been. Louise jumped to her feet. Mildred ran over to her. Thaddeus yelled, "hey," but he didn't move. Louise took two steps away, out of Samantha's reach. Mildred stood beside her friend.

"Go away," Louise said.

"I could beat the crap out of both of you," Samantha said.

"Go away," Mildred said.

Thaddeus stepped forward and stood beside Mildred.

"And we are not going to help you get home." Mildred pointed her finger at Samantha. "Go away."

Samantha looked at the wall of friends. "The school is just over there," she pointed at the trees. "I don't need your help." And she turned around and stomped off.

"I don't think that Love Magnet works," Thaddeus said when Samantha disappeared down what seemed to be a trail.

"Maybe if we hadn't lost it," said Louise.

"It never did any good against Samantha," said Mildred. "But we have to find it, or we'll never get home."

"I don't know about that," said Louise. "The Love Magnet doesn't work that way. It just makes people like you."

"But it's what brought us here," Mildred looked down at the spot where they'd landed. The grasses and wildflowers grew as thick as an animal's fur.

"Are we sure it brought us here?" Thaddeus said, "because I don't see how. And I don't think we'll ever find it."

"Well, maybe we don't need it," said Louise.

"Maybe it's just an actual magnet, right?" Thaddeus said.

"But," said Mildred, "we're here, aren't we?"

"I haven't figured that part out," Thaddeus said.

"No, no, listen," Louise said, "even if it did bring us here, which it never had the power to do in the books, we can probably get home without it. It's normal. Dorothy came by cyclone and went home by magic shoes. And then she came back by an underground cavern and a shipwreck, and went home by the magic belt. Then she came by a land yacht and went home by the magic belt but everyone else went home by a soap bubble."

"I don't think that's possible," said Thaddeus.

"Well, but there was glue in it. Anyway, you see, right? Usually you don't go back the way you got here. It's usually the belt that gets you back, either that or Santa Claus or something else."

"What about the Wizard?" said Thaddeus.

Mildred looked at Thaddeus to see if he was serious. Thaddeus looked at Louise.

"So we *don't* need the magnet?" said Mildred.

"Well, probably not, not for getting home, anyway," said Louise. "But for getting around in a foreign country, think about it. They put a deadly desert around the whole place. They make a whole point of not liking strangers."

"But in the books, you said…" said Mildred.

"Books aren't always *completely* accurate," said Louise. "They can't be because sometimes they contradict each other. And, think about it: The Shaggy Man had the magnet for a reason. He needed it."

"What if the magnet brought us here for a reason?" said Mildred after a minute.

"I don't see how that could be," said Louise.

"Magnets don't have reasons," said Thaddeus.

"Yeah, but it's magic," said Mildred.

"Unless," Louise paused, "unless it wants to go back to where it belongs. Maybe we're on a quest to find the Shaggy Man and give him back his magnet."

"So now you're agreeing the magnet *did* bring us here? You do know that's the opposite of what you said before," Thaddeus pointed out.

"See, it brought us here for a reason and we know what the reason is?" Mildred said.

"My thought is developing on the subject," Louise said.

The three hardly spoke during the next ten minutes as they circled around on their hands and knees over the same small patch of the field where they'd landed. Mildred was about to ask what Louise thought their options were if they never found the magnet when she heard the sound of talking from the direction of the woods and looked up, which caused Louise and Thaddeus to look up as well. It was Samantha. She was coming back, and she was with someone. She was still in the trees, but they could tell she was with a man, an older man. As they emerged from the trees, they could see the man had unkempt hair and a ragged beard and an even more ragged suit.

"It's the Shaggy Man," Louise whispered.

"Well, that *is* a coincidence," Mildred said.

"Who is the Shaggy Man?" Thaddeus asked.

"Not necessarily." Louise didn't know what to say to Thaddeus, so she replied to Mildred. "It's like I said. If the magnet was looking for him, of course it would land near where he was."

"Who is the Shaggy Man?" Thaddeus repeated.

"He's a bum," said Louise.

Samantha looked different, somehow. Perhaps it was that she was smiling. In fact her whole face seemed to have changed. It was as though, Mildred realized, as though she'd been

photoshopped. Her angry grump had been replaced by a smiley face. She was even laughing when she approached the three friends. Louise stood up and gestured to her friends to get off the ground.

"Wow," she said. "You're the Shaggy Man."

Samantha tried to frown at this. She wrinkled her mouth and it kind of swam around on her face a moment before her smile popped back on. "I found him in the woods," she said.

"How extraordinary." The Shaggy Man too was smiling; they could tell even under the thick whiskers. He walked toward them in the most friendly way, as though he was coming unexpectedly across very old friends he'd never thought he would see again—and then, suddenly, the smile dropped from his face. He looked disapproving, like a store owner would look if he'd caught a little kid, a kid he would have handed free candy to because he was so adorable, stealing a candy bar. He stopped. He took a step backwards. And then he smiled again, although in not quite as friendly a way.

"Outsiders in Oz once again," he said. "It is not often, no, not since the desert was put in place. How did you get here? Balloon? Airplane?" The Shaggy Man looked around, apparently to find the wreckage of a flying contraption.

"You don't like strangers?" said Louise.

"Love 'em," said the Shaggy Man, "most of the time. Was a stranger myself once."

"Love Magnet," said Mildred, and she took a step toward the Shaggy man.

"What about it?" said the Shaggy Man, taking half a step backwards. The Shaggy Man was again not smiling. In fact he looked a little miffed.

"That's how we got here," said Mildred. "It pulled us. I think it was looking for you."

"You must have lost it," said Louise.

"No," said the Shaggy Man. And he pulled from his pocket a small horseshoe magnet. It was dull and brown. And he pointed the ends in the direction of the children. Their faces brightened.

The sight of the magnet made Samantha giggle.

"Well that explains what happened to her," Louise said.

"I told you it was just a toy," said Thaddeus. "It was just some old piece of merchandizing."

"Well then how did it pull us here?" said Mildred.

"No reason why there couldn't be two of them," the Shaggy Man said, "or more than two for aught I know."

"Anyway, we lost it," said Louise. "We landed right here, and we've looked over this whole area."

The Shaggy Man thought a moment, then he waved the tines of his magnet back and forth over the area. Several feet ahead of where they were standing something jumped.

"I think you'll find it over there," said the Shaggy Man, seriously. And sure enough, about ten feet away from where they landed, just outside the circle Mildred had traced, the magnet, pulled by the one the Shaggy Man held, was moving over the top of a tuft of grass like a pet called back to its owner.

"How did it get way over there?" said Mildred, grabbing it.

"Momentum," said Thaddeus.

"Excuse me?" said Louise.

"Science," said Thaddeus with a sigh.

"Well," the Shaggy Man put the Love Magnet back in his pocket (which made the one Mildred was holding calm down). Then he raised his hand to get everyone's attention, "I have returned your friend to you. Now I will say goodbye."

"Friend?" said Thaddeus.

"Goodbye?" said Mildred.

Louise just looked puzzled.

"But," Samantha said, "aren't you going to help us?"

"I thought I was," said the Shaggy Man. "But, well, I guess I'll just say it: I don't find you at all pleasant to be around. This surprises me quite a lot, as I generally am very fond of children. I know you can't help but like me, as I have the Love Magnet. But that does not make me like you. And I don't seem to like you at all."

"You don't like us?" Samantha said.

"Well, I like *you* well enough," the Shaggy Man said to Samantha. "But your friends, I'm afraid not. I don't see any reason to mince words. I wish you well. But I don't wish to be with you.

You are in Oz, so you are not likely to be in any grave danger. At least I don't think so."

"But why don't you like us?" said Mildred.

"I cannot say why. It's just something about you." He waved and turned to go.

"But we need to find a way home," said Thaddeus.

The Shaggy Man paused and turned back. "Well, perhaps that is it. Perhaps you give off the air of children who have, as very few children ever do, made it here, to Oz, and, like a child who cries at the sight of a clown or a child who's afraid of an elephant show, you no sooner have your ticket in hand than you cry that you've had enough and want to go home. You're in Oz, for goodness sake. Why would you possibly want to go home? Have a look around."

"But... but..." said Louise, who really did want to stay and have a look around, "you're not like this."

"Books," said Thaddeus, hoping Louise would remember her own earlier comment about books.

"Stay warm and keep out of the snow, and you'll be fine." That was the last thing the Shaggy Man said as he turned on his leather heels and headed back into the woods.

"Still think this Love Magnet works?" said Thaddeus.

"Keep out of the snow?" said Louise.

"Winter's coming. He told me," said Samantha, whose smile had faded but whose new interest in the three of them apparently had not.

"It never snows in Oz," Louise continued. It's never winter in Oz. I don't ever remember anything about snow. Not even in Plumly."

"What about when the Wicked Witch..." Mildred began.

"That's the movie," Louise cut her off. "This is the real thing."

"Looks like the books aren't any more real than the movie," said Thaddeus, though he'd never seen the one or read the others.

"They can't be totally wrong," said Louise. "I am sure they're mostly fine."

"I wouldn't mind staying a while," said Mildred, "if I knew we had a way home."

Four

On his way home, a fox darted across the Shaggy Man's path. He called to it. It startled and shifted its eyes and kept running.

There had been a lot of foxes in the area lately. Were they regular Oz foxes, or had they been part of the troop the Tin Woodman and the Cowardly Lion and the Scarecrow had told him about? He wanted to know. If only he pulled the Love Magnet out of his pocket quickly enough, he might get one to talk to him. By the time he pulled it out of his shaggy pocket, the fox was gone.

When he got to his door, he noticed by the handle a number of scratch marks he hadn't noticed before. Maybe they were new, and maybe they were not. Maybe a fox had tried to get into his little home but didn't have the thumbs to turn the handle. On the other hand, it was a pretty shaggy house, made mostly of scrap wood he'd collected here and there over a long time. Maybe those scratches had always been there and only his edginess had made him see them.

He opened the door—which was not locked, it did not even have a lock—and went inside.

Maybe he'd give up his house and start back on his wandering ways, he thought. He'd never meant to stay here more than a season or so. In fact, if it had not been so cold lately, he probably would have left already. Thank goodness he'd thought to build the stone fireplace, remembering the comfort of a fire from when he was a boy in the territory, never imagining he'd need it for warmth.

But it did not appear the cold would be passing anytime soon. Every morning began with a cloudy exhale. And, although today was warm and almost normal, most days made him shiver even when the sun was up, behind a cloud of smoke and birds. Two-shirt weather it was. And two shirts was one shirt more than the Shaggy Man owned. He had never felt such a chill in Oz before. It felt the way it had felt back before he came to Oz when he used to see the world by train. It felt like Chicago at the approach of winter, when the city closed in on you and freeze-promising gales blew in from the lake.

He sat in his comfy chair and picked up a book that he opened but didn't read. He was thinking of the four children. How oddly he'd treated them. He liked children. He loved children, and they loved him. But these children, well...? It's truly the rare person who can like absolutely everyone. But was sending them off in the cold a good idea—even in Oz?

He heard a scratching sound by the window behind him. He rose up to see what it was. He heard a rustling in the trees behind the house like the sound of something running away. Then he heard a knock at the door.

"Yes?" he said, "it's not locked." He half expected to hear the scratch of a fox trying to turn the knob. But the knob turned without a sound and the door swung to.

And there in the doorway stood Scraps the Patchwork Girl, and Tik-Tok the Mechanical Man, and Professor H.M. Wogglebug, T.E.

"Well, don't that beat all," the Shaggy Man called out. "Come in, come in."

"JUST to STOP a mo-MENT," Tik-Tok said, crossing the threshold.

"The Wobbly Bug would love a nip of water or milk or any liquid you got to wash down his supper pills," Scraps said.

"That's Wog*g*lebug," said Professor Wogglebug.

"Perhaps when you say it it is," Scraps grinned.

"Wouldn't mind a rest either," the Wogglebug sat himself in a chair at the Shaggy Man's table.

"Water I've got aplenty," said the Shaggy Man.

"Kinda wish he wasn't with us," Scraps announced in a jolly tone that suggested no offense in the world. "Always needing to fill up and turn off 'stead of going on-an-on till the job is done."

The Shaggy Man chuckled. "Never knew you to take the straightest road, Scraps."

"Well, yeah, could be, but I can't take *any* road at all while he's *resting,* I've got to stop and lace and unlace my excellent fingers till he's done." And as she said it, she proceeded to braid her fingers together to see if she could get them too tangled to pull apart.

"OZ-ma MUST have had a rea-SON to send a BLOOD CREAT-ure. Our LOY-al-TY makes US TAKE him how-EV-er he SLOWS us DOWN."

"I am sure my brains do more than make up for my occasional need to rest," said the Wogglebug, "and thank you so much for the refreshment, Shaggy Man."

"What a funny time it has been," said the Shaggy Man as he sat back down in his comfy chair. "Here I've been in this house for a year with no other visitor than Jack Pumpkinhead, and now I've had the Tin Man, the Scarecrow, the Cowardly Lion, and four American children and the three of you all in a row."

"Ah, ha!" the Wogglebug exclaimed. "My thirst, you see, is proving useful. We are on a quest for the Tin Man, the Scarecrow, and the Cowardly Lion. Tell us, when did you see them, and what did they say, and where are they now?"

"What?" The Shaggy Man tapped himself on his head with his book. "You mean they're not back to the Emerald City yet? Oh, dear." And he thought of how long it would take to get to the former witch's castle and back. "They should have been back days and days ago."

"Huh," said Scraps, trying to pull her hands apart. "I'll bet they got themselves tangled up in a *some*thing. They are easily distracted, you know."

"What DID you TALK A-bout?" asked Tik-Tok.

"They told me they were on a journey to find the origin of the birds and the smoke in the old castle. And then they said they were after figuring out where the elephants and the foxes came from. I haven't seen a single elephant myself. But there have been a lot of foxes."

"No," said the Wogglebug. "No elephants, no foxes. Are you sure you heard that right?"

"Oh, I saw elephants and foxes aplenty," said the Patchwork Girl.

"YOU did?" said the clockwork man.

"Unless I just imagined them. Say, here, can anyone untie my fingers?"

"Tin Man told me that they'd stopped at all the houses on the way to hear what they could hear. And he said a farmer up the road had told him about a whole herd of elephants with foxes on their backs. And one of the foxes was wearing a crown. Of course I thought of King Dox of Foxville. But how could King Dox cross the deadly desert?"

"HOW in-DEED."

"What about the Manerikin children?" said Scraps.

"The Manerikin children?" said the Shaggy Man.

"There's no such thing as a Manerikin," said the Wogglebug.

"Oh, the American children," said the Shaggy Man.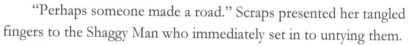

"Yes, they got past the deadly desert too, somehow."

"Perhaps someone made a road." Scraps presented her tangled fingers to the Shaggy Man who immediately set in to untying them.

"WELL we MUST be GO-ING," said Tik-Tok.

"Well, perhaps I should come with you," said the Shaggy Man.

"No, no, no," said Scraps. "We already have a bug that needs shutting down and filling up time, and a clockwork man that needs pausing to re-wind. We don't need another meat creature weighing down our skedaddling."

"PER-HAPS you MUST STAY in CASE they RE-TURN. WE shall DO OZ-ma's BID-DING."

"Well, perhaps I can't add anything to the team you don't already have at that," said the Shaggy Man.

"Oh, yeah," said Scraps. "But how about you give old Tik-Tok a twist on his key holes before we go. None of us has the twistisity to do that." She rolled her hands over each other as she spoke.

"Oh, sure, pleasure," said the Shaggy Man. And he located the mechanical man's key and wound up his thoughts and his speech and his action good and tight before waving goodbye.

Almost as soon as they were out of sight, the Shaggy Man heard another scratching at the back window of his house and he rushed to it in time to see the white tip of fox's tail disappear through the underbrush.

Five

"She doesn't seem like a coward."

"Excuse me," said Louise.

"My mother said that bullies are really just cowards," Mildred said, "but Samantha doesn't seem like a coward. She keeps wandering off alone in a strange place when she could just stay safe with us."

"I don't think we make people safe exactly," said Thaddeus.

"You want her to stay with us?" Louise asked.

"We brought her here. Aren't we responsible for her now?"

"But you said you weren't going to help her," said Thaddeus. "And why should we? She wants to beat us up."

"I was in a lather," Mildred said. It was an expression of her mother's. She wasn't sure what it meant, but this seemed like the time to use it. "It's not a good idea to hang on to that stuff when you calm down."

"Well I don't see any reason to help her," Thaddeus said. "And I don't think she wants to be helped."

Samantha had wandered off for the second time almost as soon as the Shaggy Man left them. It turned out there was a dirt road not far from where they'd landed, hidden from view by the tall grass. It led them away from the woods where the Shaggy Man lived. Samantha had taken off down it in a fast trot.

"That's not the point," said Mildred. "I don't like her either. But what happens if we go home and she stays here?"

"Works for me," said Louise.

"She'll be stuck here," said Mildred, "and we'll get in trouble."

"You don't know she'd be stuck. People always get home if they want to," said Louise.

"In the books," said Thaddeus.

"And if she's with us, she'll just boss us around," Louise added, avoiding Thaddeus, who was staring at her.

"She shouldn't wander off alone," said Mildred.

"That doesn't mean she's not a coward," said Thaddeus.

Mildred looked at him for several seconds. "Well *I* wouldn't do it," she said at last.

"Depends on what she's scared of most—us or this place."

"I don't think she's scared of us," said Louise. "She was going to stomp on my back."

"You think that means she *isn't* scared of you?" said Thaddeus.

"I'll ask my mother about it when we get home," Mildred said.

The afternoon was wearing on. And the air was just detectably chillier. The day seemed to pass slowly in Oz, but evening would come eventually, and they should be ready for it. Mildred rubbed her arms. Thaddeus said they should think where they would spend the night, but then he also said they shouldn't just wander up to a stranger's door and ask for things unless they absolutely had to. So Mildred didn't know what he wanted.

"Where are we going, exactly?" Thaddeus asked. "How did Dorothy know where to go in all those books?"

"She just tended to wander around until she ran into someone who could help her," Louise said. "Obviously we'd be best off finding Ozma in the Emerald City, but usually you have to find some other people and have some adventures first."

"But those are just books, like you said before. So who knows?" said Mildred.

"I'm sure they're mostly right," said Louise. "Otherwise what would be the point?"

"And the Emerald City is in this direction?" Thaddeus pointed in the direction they were going.

"I think so," said Louise.

"You *think* so?"

"Well, the maps in the books reverse east and west. And that's confusing. Maybe in Oz they really are reversed. Maybe here the sun sets in the east, and maybe the east is where the west is supposed to be."

"Huh?" said Thaddeus.

"Wouldn't that just mean it sets in the west like normal?" Mildred asked.

Louise said, "I said it was confusing. All I know is we have to go east to get to Emerald City. I just don't know if that means that we go toward the setting sun or away from it."

Thaddeus tried to work that out. "This is still Earth, right?" he said.

"We'd better ask someone," said Louise.

"We don't know anyone," said Mildred.

"What's that got to do with it?" asked Thaddeus.

"But you said..." Mildred begin.

"We're not asking for stuff. We're asking for directions."

"Just be careful," said Mildred. "You never know who's going to answer a door."

Soon they came upon a small dwelling, yellow-gold; it was round like an igloo but with a regular door and a chimney on each side. The doors and window looked a little like a face—and not a very friendly one. Mildred stood behind the others as the door was swung open by a little woman in a yellow dress and pointed hat.

"No, I don't think so," the woman in the yellow dress said as soon as Louise explained their situation and asked for some water.

"We're lost," said Thaddeus.

The woman looked them up and down suspiciously without saying anything.

"Maybe we should just go," Mildred said, taking a step back.

The woman nodded at this and closed the door firmly and then, for good measure, pulled in the shutters on the nearest window. Mildred took a step back, but Louise and Thaddeus did not move.

"Who was it?" a deeper voice just beyond the door said.

"The beggars," said the woman.

Louise looked open-mouthed at her two friends. "But this is Oz. And we have the Love Magnet."

Mildred drew it out of her pocket. "This is why I don't talk to people. We're just going to have to figure this out on our own."

"Did you see Samantha in there?" said Thaddeus. "She was inside, sitting at a table. I think she was eating. And that's just a toy."

"It *pulled* us here," Mildred reminded Thaddeus—again.

"That must explain it, though," said Louise. "It's a strong magnet. But Samantha must have told them lies about us in case we showed up. And now they hate us."

"But…" said Thaddeus.

"Think about it," said Louise. "If the hate is stronger than the magnet, it wouldn't work, would it? Not all the way, I mean."

"Though I would have thought Oz people were supposed to be a little nicer than that. You know, 'jolly ole land of Oz,'" said Mildred.

"Well, that's just a movie," said Louise.

Just then the door opened again. This time a small man stood in the doorway. He had a wispy beard, all grey and white, and an oversized nose. He, like the woman, was all dressed in yellow. He wore overalls and a round hat with small decorative bells hanging off the brim. He turned his head away from the children without talking to them and continued his conversation with the woman behind the door. "I don't know what's gotten in to you today. Visitors who need help, and you don't..." He cut himself off as he turned back at the children. "Oh," he said pushing his mustache into his nose with his lip as though he were trying to keep out a bad smell. "I see what you mean." He looked the children up and down but apparently found nothing he liked.

The three children craned their heads to see past him. And there indeed was Samantha sitting at the table in front of a bowl of soup. She glanced their way for just a second without making eye contact, acting as though she hadn't seen them at all.

"Hey, Samantha," Louise yelled in. "That wasn't very..."

"I'll just be closing the door now," the little man said. "Be on your way."

"But we're very thirsty," said Thaddeus, "and it's getting cold."

"There's a stream out back if you must," said the Winkie man, "fresh, sweet water." And he closed the door.

"How's that supposed to help with the cold?" said Thaddeus.

Before they got to the stream, the smell of smoke tainted the air and made the children turn their heads. It wasn't coming from the little yellow house but from much farther away. Across the stream in the direction of the high hills. A black stain undulated in a stain of orange smoke. It started from one particular hill and spread across the whole sky. This hill was closer than the rest but still quite far off. The girls stared. Thaddeus knelt down at the bank to figure out how to get a good drink from this clear, fast moving water. It wasn't really a stream at all. It was a river—wide enough for a boat. He reached his hand into the water to scoop a drink. All the water leaked through his fingers before he could pull his hand to his mouth.

"What are those," Mildred was pointing at the cloud. It was growing thicker as it drew closer and in it holes began to appear, opening and closing in the orange stain.

Thaddeus laid his body flat on the bank and pushed his head as close to the water as he could and reached in again with his cupped hand. The water was warm, which was strange. It takes longer for water to cool down than air. But this water felt a lot warmer than the air.

"They're birds," said Louise.

Lots of birds. As the cloud drew closer, the orange stain lightened in places. And a sound drifted down. A twittering.

Thaddeus was too thirsty to think much about anything but getting the water to his lips. But he couldn't keep the water in his cupped hand long enough to drink it. He slunk his body closer to the surface, grabbing tight with one hand to the rushes that grew on the bank to keep himself from falling into the river.

The twittering, mild and almost pleasant at first, grew louder as the birds got closer. The tuft Thaddeus was holding ripped away. The twittering of the birds grew so loud, the girls put their hands over their ears. Thaddeus tumbled into the water. The girls did not hear the splash.

"That's really annoying," Mildred tried to yell, but Louise couldn't hear her above the cacophony of screaming birds.

The swift river pulled Thaddeus far from the bank before he could come up for air. Then it carried him away as though it were an animal and he was its food.

Six

The trees were thick between the travelers and their destination. The back-lit black castle sat like a solid shadow above a cloud of dark green leaves. Soon the shadow would sink below the cloud and into the forest as Scraps, Tik-Tok, and the Wogglebug got nearer to the trees and entered the woods. There, they'd need another way to find it, as there had not been any paths worn in that direction for many years. The smoke wouldn't help. It was no longer billowing from the top of the dark mountain. It had gone from orange to green and then stopped altogether. Overhead, the flock of birds had squawked uproariously as it retreated to the castle, leaving the cold behind but returning to the sky its natural blue. But now the blue felt sad, somehow. At least if felt that way to the Wogglebug, although he would not say so.

Tik-Tok informed his companions, now that things were getting serious and decisions may have to be made, that he was the leader of the expedition. He was, after all, the entire Grand Army of Oz, having been given the job by Ozma herself. There was no point in H. M. Wogglebug T. E.'s arguing about it. All the Wogglebug had was brains. Tik-Tok had authority. The professor huffed but did not argue. He was too cold for that. And as for Scraps, she saw no reason to argue. She didn't care who the leader was, as long as she was free to do whatever she liked whenever she wanted to.

"WELL," said Tik Tok, "one MYS-ter-y HAS been SOLVED."

"Of course it has," said the Wogglebug, pulling his wrap closer around his insect body. "In fact any number have been solved. Positively dozens, I'm sure. But which one were you referring to, Captain?"

"The COL-ors OF the SMOKE. GREEN for GO, OR-ange for COME back."

"Brilliant," sang Scraps. "Green for go, orange for come back—and black for whatever black is for."

"That?" said the Wogglebug. "Haven't we always known about the colors?"

Scraps stopped. She leaned like a mime upon an imaginary tree. "We knew?"

The Wogglebug stopped beside her. "Of course we did." He put an appendage under his chin and raised his complicated eyeballs at the sky. "How could we not?"

"Oh, I'm all kinds of knots," Scraps rubbed a hand across her quilted body, "but what are these dozens of mysteries we've already solved? What else do we know?"

"It were tedious to catalog all we know. I'm sure when the time comes…"

"What is the black smoke for?" Scraps asked.

"Well, the black smoke…" the Wogglebug paused.

"And what kind of birds are those? And who is sending them? And are they wild birds or pet birds? And who is in the broken castle? And why is who there? And what happened to the Scarecrow and the Tin Woodman and the Lion after they left the Shaggy Man's darling little hovel? And…"

"I think we should catch up to Tik-Tok," said the Wogglebug pointing to the Grand Army of Oz who had not slowed down for the discussion.

"WE will CON-tin-UE by THE most DI-rect ROUTE from HERE," said Tik-Tok as soon as the others had caught up. "WE MUST stay on the SAME line we WERE ON WHEN we first ENTered THE WOODS."

"Yes, we will, and yes, we must," said Scraps. "Who cares if the Shaggy Man told us to beware? And who cares if the most direct route is the one they'll be most on the lookout for trespassers on? Be bold and straight and all that."

The Wogglebug pointed out that what the Shaggy Man had actually said was "be careful."

Having crossed the field by a path that had turned to thick grass, they entered the woods. The light was dim, but there was plenty still left—perhaps enough to get to the castle before dark. Hard as it would be to find their way in daylight, they would certainly not be able to find it in the dark. This made the Patchwork Girl giddy. "Won't it be fun to see how far we travel with nothing to see and where we will come out in the morning?" she giggled.

"in-E-fic-CIENT," said Tik-Tok.

"Oh, I do hope so," said Scraps.

"Well, hmm. As jolly as that game sounds," said the Wogglebug, "some of us do have to sleep at night."

"You and who else?"

The Wogglebug took a deep breath to prepare his reply, but before he got a chance to exhale, the Patchwork Girl was pointing at something behind a tree and marching off, bum out, in the direction of her finger. "What is that?"

It was a doorframe, sitting in the woods, empty on both sides. You could open the door, as she did, and walk right through both ways.

"Funniest thing I ever saw today," she said. "Do you suppose the house was torn down and carted away?"

The Wogglebug really wasn't curious. But thinking this might be an opportunity to show off his deductive skills, he said, or began to say, "If you look carefully at what would be the circumference or rather the area of a…"

"Perhaps we should knock," said Scraps.

"Why would we do that?" asked the professor.

"See if anyone's home."

"EX-quis-ITE i-DE-a," said Tik-Tok, reaching out his hand and hitting solidly on the door.

"I can't imagine what you think you're going to…" the Wogglebug said. But just then he heard a noise, a noise like a machine makes when it is starting up. And seconds later the ground behind the door opened up, and out of the ground rose a box, snug against the frame. The door opened. And staring at them from the other side was a little man, a little taller than a Winkie but no taller than the Grand Army of Oz.

"Well, welcome." He spoke with an unfamiliar accent. But his words were cheery. He held out his hand. The hand seemed to be made of metal. Either that or he was wearing a metal glove. In fact both of his hands and his feet, along with his knees, elbows and shoulders were either made of metal or encased in it. He wore a metal hat with a funnel top and flaps that covered his ears.

"Welcome, welcome, clockwork man, quilted woman, and highly magnified bug-person. Do be coming in," he said. "I am called Tin-Puh."

"Tin who?" said the professor.

"Puh," said the man.

"Oh, Pooh," said Scraps, the syllable exploding from her lips. "I get it. Lovely, lovely, lovely," and she jumped into the box, beckoning the others.

Seven

Mildred had to stop. She and Louise had been running all this way and not getting any closer to Thaddeus who was still caught in the swift current of the river. He was far out of reach and almost out of sight. They yelled at him. He yelled back. They yelled, "swim this way." Mildred yelled, "try to go under the water." Maybe the current wasn't as strong down below. He yelled, "It's pulling me too hard. I can't move." But he didn't hear what they yelled, and they couldn't hear what he yelled back, only the far-away sound of his voice. He didn't seem to be in any danger. He wasn't struggling. He was just floating like a stick.

"I can't run anymore," Mildred panted.

"But Thaddeus…" Louise grabbed Mildred's arm and pointed downstream. "Well, that's weird."

"What's weird?"

"He stopped."

Thaddeus hadn't gotten any further away. He was floating in place.

"Okay," said Mildred, and she took a step forward.

Thaddeus moved again—about the distance of a step. Mildred and Louise started to run again. Thaddeus started to move again. They stopped. He stopped.

"Huh?" said Louise.

"That's just weird," said Mildred.

Thaddeus noticed the same thing, "What's going on?" he yelled.

"Oz is weird," Louise yelled back. She remembered how the Shaggy Man got his donkey head replaced by his real head by taking a dip in the Truth Pond in *The Road to Oz*.

"Yeah, I guess it is," said Mildred.

Now that he was no longer being pulled by the current, Thaddeus tried to swim toward them. But the river held him in place, somehow. He didn't feel a pull or push in any direction. The river flowed gently past him as though he were anchored where he was. And yet he was floating.

Louise had an idea. "If we're pushing him away by walking toward him, then maybe we can pull him back by walking away from him. Or, or maybe we could pull him to the bank by walking away from the river."

They took several steps away from the water. Then they took several steps upstream. Thaddeus stayed where he was. And worse than that, he was starting to struggle to stay afloat.

"This is freaking me out," he yelled, trying to swim one way and then another to find a way the stream would allow him to go.

"That's it," Louise said. "I'm going to go get him." And she pulled off her shoes.

"You can't go get him, that's dangerous."

"I'm a better swimmer than he is."

"But it's cold."

Louise pulled off her jeans and jumped in.

"It's not cold," she said as the river started to pull her away.

"Well if you're going in, I'm going in." Mildred jumped in too.

The water was comfortably warm, as though it was heated. That was odd. But it was funnier than that. As soon as Louise had hit the water, she felt herself held up, buoyant was the word, like a cork and at the same time pushed or pulled downstream toward Thaddeus, though Thaddeus himself was no longer struggling and not getting any farther away. Getting to him was going to be easy in this water. But as soon as Mildred entered the water, the pull or the push stopped. The water grew suddenly thicker, sort of, anyway harder to swim in and more of a struggle to stay afloat in—as though it had become thicker and thinner at the same time.

This was an advantage for Thaddeus. He adjusted his body and paddled himself toward the bank. And it wasn't a problem for Louise either. She was a very good swimmer. But it was not at all good for Mildred.

"A little help." Mildred was kicking hard to keep her head out of the water. She felt herself being tugged down. She had to gulp air.

Louise had made it to the bank when she heard Mildred struggle. She jumped back in, grabbed her friend, wrapping an arm under her armpit and across her chest the way they'd taught her to in swimming class and together they kicked their way back to safety.

Mildred coughed.

"You're lucky I took lessons," said Louise. "I thought you were a better swimmer than that."

"It was pulling me down."

"Your jeans were pulling you down," said Louise. "They're full of water."

"That may not be it," said Thaddeus.

"They teach you that in lifesaving," Louise said.

"But we're outside. And he's a boy," said Mildred.

"You can't save other people if you're drowning," Louise said.

"I don't think the stuff they teach you is going to be a lot of help here," said Thaddeus.

"That's because it's magic," said Louise.

"I don't know about that. But some things don't work the way you expect them to," Thaddeus said.

"You still don't think it's magic?" said Mildred. "You were just in it."

"Everything looks like magic until you understand it," said Thaddeus. "But it is…" and he paused several seconds. He looked at the swift, wide river, the distant purple mountains, cloud topped, with the sun standing on top of them. It all looked like the sort of thing you might see anywhere. "…weird," he said. "But I'm sure there's a real explanation, like a hot spring or something."

"And then what made you move when we moved?" said Louise. "Didn't it feel like magic."

"Card tricks feel like magic until someone explains them," said Thaddeus.

Louise didn't know what to say. She looked to Mildred for help. But Mildred didn't know what to say or even what to believe. She decided she'd have to talk some things over with her mother later. She said, "I'm just cold." As soon as they were on dry land, the cold had dashed in. Mildred felt as though she'd strapped bags of icy sand to her thighs. Louise grabbed Mildred's arm and pulled her along the towpath.

Thaddeus was trying to squeeze the water from his shirt and pants. "I was more comfortable in the river."

They were all cold and wet and thoroughly exercised, and the afternoon had turned to evening. There was plenty to talk about and plenty of reason to get mad at Thaddeus for falling into the river, but as soon as Mildred had said it, they all agreed those things had to wait. Thaddeus wondered if they should climb back into the river where they could at least be warm. But Louise pointed out that would only delay the getting dry, which was just as important as being warm, and they couldn't stay in the river all night because they'd have to sleep. And by then the air would be even colder. Mildred suggested they return to the house of the little old couple, who could not be so hard hearted as to leave them outdoors in the cold. But Louise pointed out the air was not so cold that they were in danger of freezing and although they were hungry, they were not starving. Also, the incident with the river had taken them pretty far from the farmer's house.

"Yeah, but they are the only people we've seen since that bum," said Mildred.

Thaddeus and Louise believed they'd be more likely to find help by moving forward than going back.

"This is Oz," Louise said. "It's a fairy land. Someone always helps."

Thaddeus looked as though he were going to say something. He raised his hand as though to use it to make a point. But then he lowered it and shrugged.

"Well the books can't be completely wrong," Louise said as though she'd heard what Thaddeus hadn't said.

They kept to the path that ran along the river.

Soon, behind them, came the sound of a bell, actually two bells,

dull, syncopated thuds, accompanied by a higher maaa-maaa-maaaaah and a lower maaa-maa-maaah, almost like singing. A pair of goats was coming down the path with bells on their bobbing necks and a harness and a rope. The rope was tied to a little boat in the middle of the river which had a little structure like a house sitting in the middle. There was a little old woman on deck in a long red dress hiked up to her knees and a matching pointed hat. She was holding a long pole. She didn't seem to notice the children. Thaddeus waved. She did not wave back.

The children ran to the goats who slowed down and raised their heads and seemed to smile. The animals stopped to accept petting. The old woman in the dull dress put a hand on her hip and yelled to the shore. "Hey, you there, don't you know what the bell is for?

'Back off' and 'get outta the way.' You think it means, 'come crash my boat'? You know what happens if those goats stop?"

"Sorry," Thaddeus yelled back.

"Nothing happens if we stop," said the first goat in what sounded like a husky woman's voice.

"The boat swings around and bangs into the river bank," said the second goat in a higher-pitched male voice. "That's something."

Upon hearing goats speak, Thaddeus's face contorted into the face of someone who'd just taken a big bite of a particularly pungent onion. But no one saw the face, and he didn't say anything.

"Keep petting," said the first goat. "Long way from the Great Sandy Waste."

"You walked all the way from…"

"…the Castle of Glinda the Good," the first goat finished Louise's sentence.

"You're giving away secrets again," said the other goat.

"Through the Emerald City, then on to here," the first goat said. "Need a pet."

And then from the water came the voice of the woman in the red dress: "I'll thank you not to talk to my goats while they're working." She was pulling herself and the boat toward the bank, hand over hand along the rope.

"She's a witch, but she's harmless," said the first goat. "More pets."

"So *you* say," said the second goat, bracing himself against the strong tug of the rope.

"Who's harmless?" Louise asked.

"Witch Lloco-Monnem," said the first goat.

"Loco-what?" said Thaddeus.

"Lloco-Monnem," said the second goat. "She's a witch. And she's not *exactly* harmless—exactly."

"All right then," the little woman in the soiled dress called as she pulled, "if you're going to slow me down and eat up my time, I think I have a right to know your names, do I not?"

"Maybe we'd better just go," Thaddeus whispered. "She thinks she's a witch."

"Remember, there are good witches and bad witches in Oz," said Louise. "So that doesn't tell us anything."

"Probably middle witches too," said Mildred, "not good or bad. Just regular."

By then the boat was at the river bank. The witch was a small, broad woman with a wrinkled, flat face. "Yes, I do. Oh, look, shiverers, get on the boat, now, now, now. Why did I even do this? Mumps people, are you? Yes, of course, must be. Not Oz people." No one knew what she meant. But she just kept talking, "No, no, names later. Someone might see us." With a jerk of her head she pulled the children aboard. Moments later, she had them standing around an unlit, black stove in the cramped and cluttered little cabin. Mildred started to thank her, but the woman cut her off. "Not a word until you're warm and dry. Can't you see I'm busy, little girl? My stars, if I live to be eight thousand and twelve I'll never know what good comes from children." Lloco-Monnem pointed from one head to another with her arm fully extended. The end of her draping sleeve was frayed and streaked black with oil or coal dust. As she spoke, she was loading the little stove first with paper, then with kindling, and finally with lumps of coal. She picked up a jar on a shelf. Above the jar hung a pointed black hat that looked

a lot like the soiled red hat the witch was wearing and seemed to be full of something as though it were a bag. It was hard to tell what was in it, sort of an ashy powder, like dust, or like the leavings of a vacuum cleaner. When she lifted it to move it out of the way, a little cloud rose above the brim.

"Well, that's odd," she said as the cloud grew thick and she pulled a string to close the top tight. As the boat moved forward, the tawny cloud of smoke or dirt moved back and a little sideways until it settled over Mildred. "Odder, still," said the witch. Mildred coughed and waved her hands and blew the cloud away.

Lloco-Monnem looked the children up and down again, more carefully this time. But saying nothing, she opened the jar with pinholes in the lid and reached a little gnarly hand inside and grabbed something in her fist and yanked it out. She slammed the lid back on the jar. "Wasting a firefly on you," she said as she flicked her fist at the opening of the stove, spreading her fingers to hurl the insect inside and then quickly dropping the black cover down. Moments later the fire was blazing and warmth was filling the room like an expanding balloon.

"Was that an actual firefly?" Mildred asked.

"What other kind of firefly is there?" The witch held up the glass jar. "And I don't have many left and this is not the time of year for hunting them either. You see the problem?"

"They're not reusable?" asked Louise.

"They're not re-catchable," said the witch who was carefully returning the black hat to its place on the shelf. "Now tell me your story, and leave out the dumb parts. No wait, if you're dumb enough to be cold and wet, what are the chances you know how to tell a story? Mumps find you, or Tin-Puh maybe? Go as far as we can by boat, have to walk the final leg."

"Well, actually," Mildred began. But the Witch Lloco-Monnem didn't appear to have any real interest in hearing what the children might have to say.

"I suppose you're hungry. Yes, you are. Hang on. No, don't sit down until you're... Hey," she paused and looked at Louise. "How come you're not as wet as the others?"

"Because..."

"Never mind, not curious about that. Not curious about anything. Just don't sit down until you can do it without leaving butt marks on the wood."

"Yeah, Louise, but how come your pants are dry?" Thaddeus hadn't noticed before.

"Because I'm not an idiot," said Louise, she was looking at Mildred.

"I was in a hurry," said Mildred.

Witch Lloco-Monnem paused in her gathering of food, turned and screwed up her mouth.

"Why were you at Glinda's palace?" Louise asked.

"Quadling," she said, pointing to her red dress with both hands.

"I can see that," Louise said. "But..."

"Oh, so you want details. Mumps sent me," she said. "I mean it was my idea. We had to shut down that magic book, didn't we?"

"Glinda has a magic book that tells her what's going on everywhere," Louise explained.

"Who you talking to?" asked the witch. "No, no. Keep it to yourself. Brilliant bit of magic we worked up to solve that sticky little problem. Dust helped." She tapped the hat. "Foxes found the spell. Now she reads her book, it tells her just only what she wants to hear: same ole, same ole. Oz as always, corner to corner, dull and cheerful." And the witch cackled as though she'd made a joke. The children just looked at each other. The witch went on as though they were laughing at her story. "Then onto the Emerald City. Had a key they said, special made, would unlock the palace. Turns out it wasn't even locked. Not much security in this country. Too friendly for its own good. Walked right into the princess's boudoir and turned off that magic picture. Dust helped with that too."

This time she didn't laugh, but she smiled a menacing smile and tapped the hatful of dust a second time. Her accomplice. The children did not respond in kind to the witch's gleeful bragging. Another puff of tawny smoke exhaled from the tightly closed hat and curled a path like a beckoning finger to Mildred.

"What's with the hat?" Louise asked.

The old woman shifted her eyes. She put her hand on the brim and looked at the children as though she was dying to tell them more. She put a finger to her lip and said, "You are Mumps' people, aren't you? I feel that you are, felt it from the middle of the river. So why aren't you laughing?" They just stared at her until she said, "How'd you end up in the river anyway?"

Mildred told her about the people who wouldn't give them any food or water.

"Winkies," she said, "not half as friendly as what you hear." And then she looked at the floor and then back up. "You didn't tell them you were Mumps' people, did you?" When the children just looked confused, she answered her own question: "No, of course. Not even children could be that stupid. You are from Mumps, right?"

"Sure," said Louise. It seemed like the safest thing to say at the moment. Mildred and Thaddeus just glanced over at her.

Thaddeus told Lloco-Monnem how he'd fallen into the river trying to get a drink. And Louise told her about the odd magic of the river and how she and Mildred had jumped in to rescue him.

"Hmm," she said, looking at Louise, "So you're the one that's *not* the idiot? What were you going to do when you reached this one, assuming that you actually made it to him?"

Louise looked confused. "I took lifesaving."

"You think you're strong enough to pull him and yourself to the bank when he can't even pull himself out of the current? Yes? No? I didn't think so."

"Well, *she* could've rusted the Love Magnet," Louise said.

"The what?" the witch looked up from the pan she was filling with beans and sausage.

"She's got a Love Magnet," Louise said.

Mildred reached into her pocket to pull it out, but the witch raised her hand and said, "No, no, no. Keep it where it is. I know all about Love Magnets. Don't need to see it." Then she glanced back at the hat. And then at the children. She looked confused.

"Yeah, how come you don't love us?" said Louise.

"Maybe it's not a strong enough magnet to overcome the pull of stupid," she said, cutting the sausage. "I don't even like you. That's how I know you belong to Mumps."

"It's not polite to call people stupid," said Mildred.

"You got a better word for thinking you're twice as strong as a river?"

"Learning from mistakes makes you smart," Mildred pointed out. "But when you make someone feel bad for making a mistake, you steal the lesson they could have learned, and *that* is what makes people stupid."

The witch chuckled. "Don't see how a drowned person can learn anything." She turned around, "go on, turn your behinds toward the stove so you'll be dry enough to sit on my pine benches."

The witch was not the sort of person you could easily argue with. They did what she said. Steam rose off their wet clothes, and by the time the sausage and beans were heated on the little stove, the children were sitting and the windows were open.

"So now will you tell us about the hat?" Louise asked.

"Taking it to Mumps of course."

"Mumps?" said Mildred, forgetting she was supposed to be pretending to know who that was.

"Huh?" The witch looked hard at Mildred, then Louise, then Thaddeus. "You're not Mumps' people at all, are you? You don't know the Sorceress Lady Mumps. But you're not Oz people either. Well what *are* you doing here in the Mumpslands?"

"What are the Mumpslands?"

"Thought maybe you were elephant drivers. I thought, I mean, I heard they need more elephant drivers to clear the nasty old trees that stole back the grasslands after she died." The old witch made a gesture with her head in the direction of the black hat. "So many foxes pulling up lame. Elephants too for that matter."

The kids looked back with baffled expressions.

"Is that the dust of the Wicked Witch of the West?" said Louise.

Lloco-Monnem jumped back as though the question was a rock she had to dodge. "No, no, no. Why would you say that?"

"I recognized the hat. It's like all the other ones, but there's no bells. And it's black, just like hers."

And then Lloco-Monnem's tone changed again, so fast it seemed as though some other person had been poured into her body. She smiled an unfriendly smile. "Are you done eating yet?"

They had hardly had a bite.

Louise picked up a piece of sausage with her fork and looked at it. "Where do you get sausage in Oz?" she asked.

The woman shot a startled glance at Louise, the sort of glance you'd shoot at someone who had accused you of stealing a cookie that no one saw you steal.

"What?" she said.

"Nothing," said Louise. And she added, as though in explanation, "They're just books."

"Nice to be warm and dry and well fed, I'm sure," the little woman said. "Time to go."

Thaddeus thanked the woman awkwardly and then Mildred thanked her too.

"You can be a little gruff, but you're really quite nice, aren't you?" Thaddeus said.

"Not that I know of. Mistook you for elephant drivers. I don't need lost children and their Love Magnets attracting attention, that's for sure."

"What?" said Thaddeus.

"And that is why I refuse to throw you into the river, no matter what that hat is telling me. And that's that," said the woman, as she pulled the plates away from them. "Safest thing to do is put you ashore where I found you."

"It's cold outside," said Louise.

"And it's getting late," said Thaddeus.

"And it might snow. And if you fall back into the river, that's not my fault." The woman squinted from one to another. "Anyway, no one's likely to find you before tomorrow and by then it won't matter."

Mildred looked at Louise as though she expected Louise to say something. But Louise said nothing.

"The truth is, I find you irritating," said the witch. "I find each of you irritating in your own special little kiddie way."

"But, but, but," said Mildred. Louise put her hand on Mildred's arm.

"We'll be fine," Louise said. "Please, just take us to the shore."

Mildred and Thaddeus both looked at her like she was crazy.

The little witch whistled for her goats to stop and pulled the boat near the towpath and made them jump onto the land. It was a long jump, but she wouldn't pull the boat any closer. The children took a step back and then jumped for all they were worth. They scrambled onto the bank and watched the boat drift back to the middle of the river.

"What is going on?" Mildred said out loud.

"No talking to my goats," yelled the witch as the goats pulled the boat away.

"I know she's weird, but I hardly got to eat anything," Thaddeus said.

"Oz people don't eat sausage," Louise said.

"They don't?" said Thaddeus. "Are they Muslim?"

"They don't eat any animals. Not even fish. Animals talk in Oz. It would be like eating people."

"And she has a hat full of the actual dust of the Wicked Witch of the West. That can't be good, and..."

"Witches aren't real," Thaddeus said.

"In Oz they are," said Mildred.

"We should find out who this Mumps is," said Louise.

"Why would we want to do that?" Mildred asked.

"We should be careful who we talk to," said Thaddeus. "Something's going on."

"Because in all of the books, before you can go home, you have to have an adventure," Louise said to Mildred. "This is probably our adventure."

"But those are just stories," said Thaddeus.

"But what else do we have to go on?" said Mildred. "I say we do it."

Eight

The rooms and tunnels of Tin-Puh's underground snaked in all directions. The place seemed to be larger and grander and snakier than even the underground lair of the Nome King. Maybe it lay under the whole Land of Oz. And did it go farther still? Did it crawl beneath the Deadly Desert into Ev and Ix and Burzee? Is that how Tin-Puh got to Oz? It appeared massive. Tin-Puh led the citizens of Oz through hall after hall and chamber after chamber where foxes in white coats stood on their hind legs and carved away the walls with tools strapped to their paws, packing the scraped debris into carts and hauling it away. The foxes chattered as they worked, although none of them was saying anything intelligible.

As he led them through the many halls, Tin-Puh described his operation using many words but giving very little information. He talked about the size of rooms and the methods of carving and the calculations that assured the structural integrity of the ceilings and how much power was needed to keep the artificial lights on. (The Wogglebug was very interested in the artificial lights.) But he never got around to letting them know why he was doing all this carving and tunnel making or who he was or how long he'd been working down here out of the sunlight, or why he was showing them his work, or where they were going or where he had come from. He did mention the funny name of a certain sorceress whom he called "Lady Mumps," several times. But he seemed to think they already knew who this Lady Mumps was. Tin-Puh was saying so many things so fast, it was hard to decide which one to ask about. At one point he showed them a map of Oz with an outline of his network of tunnels and a big, red dot that said "CAPITAL" somewhere east of the center. He seemed very proud of his map.

"I could be scaring your Ozma with this map, no?"

"Why would you want to do that?" Scraps laughed. But Tin-Puh poked her with a glance and said nothing.

Eventually Tik-Tok managed to ask him what he was doing in Oz, but all got back was, "I must find the rest of your Woodsman."

"The rest?" said the Wogglebug.

"The body, I am meaning."

Eventually the Wogglebug started to suspect that the massive size of this underground might really be an illusion and that the map had been shown to them to make them think it had a much greater reach than it actually had. After he and his companions had been pulled through the cavern for quite a while, on the promise of rest and refreshment (two things only one of them had any use for), the Wogglebug suspected a trick of light and design by which all the rooms looked different depending on what door you entered by and the way the artificial lights shined on them, so that you could walk around in circles in a small space and think you were going and going and going. He was about to make this observation aloud when several things occurred to him all at once: the first was that he was cold, even colder down here than he had been above ground, and,

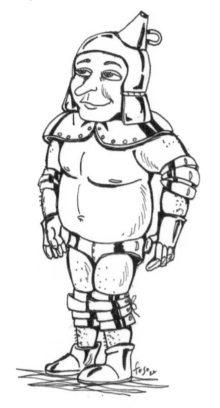

being a bug, being cold made things difficult, things like moving and speaking and thinking. He'd used so much energy wandering through these rooms, that he had almost none left with which to speak. The second thing was that he was hungry. (He had food pills aplenty in one of the large pockets of his jacket, but he had no water to wash them down with.) The third and fourth things were that he was thirsty and tired. And the fifth and last thing, which showed him that despite these five things, his magnified brain was still in fine order, was that if this was a trick, then Tin-Puh was the trickster. And whatever the reason for the trickery was, it probably would not be a good idea to let on that he'd figured out that they were being tricked.

Perhaps he would just whisper his suspicion to Tik-Tok.

"¡ OB-serve that YOU are in DEEP CON-tem-PLA-TION," Tik-Tok said under the chatter of Tin-Puh when the Wogglebug tapped him on the shoulder.

"Oh," said Tin-Puh, pausing in his explanation of the perfect ratio of cotton to carbon in a dust mask, raising a metal or metal-shelled finger and running it across the cavern wall and gouging a path in the salt like something a worm would make. "And would the large insect care in kindness to share deep thoughts with Tin-Puh?"

"I am merely admiring your work," the professor replied without a pause.

"for MY-self I say that TIN-PUH is NOT as he AP-PEARS. i SUS-pect de-CEP-tion."

The Wogglebug laughed.

"Really?" said Scraps. "That would be thrilling, wouldn't it? What's the plan Tin-Puh? You gonna lock us in the vault and steal the gold? If only we had gold. Or a vault."

The Wogglebug laughed again. "Mechanical brains and batting," he said.

"FIRST your map. DO YOU fiz-i-DIG-le cum-so-LUT-ing hy-ber-HOB-ble in-TU-ZIB-ick-IAH—."

"Oh, dear, his speech has run down," said the Wogglebug.

"Makes perfect sense to me," said Scraps, who looked at Tik-Tok and bowed, "WO-gee DONG-sur-KEY JHE-U-shwoh-AH-le."

"That doesn't mean anything," said the Wogglebug.

"Maybe not to you," she replied. "But I'm sure it says something to somebody."

"We just need to wind up his speech," said the Wogglebug. Among them only Tin-Puh had the strength and dexterity for that.

"No time is," said Tin-Puh. "Nothing for him to be saying just now, no? No, no, not at all. Let him to jabber jabber. I am having a room here I die to show you."

The Wogglebug felt the short hairs on the back of his head stick up like porcupine quills. "Only take a moment," he said, and he took the key from under Tik-Tok's arm and pushed it into the slot on his copper head embossed with the word "SPEECH." Tin-Puh looked back with a scowl that jumped immediately into a strained smile, like an animal who couldn't decide on the best way to avoid a hunter. He crossed and uncrossed his arms as he tried to force his face into a more suitable expression. The Patchwork Girl stood on her head.

"From where I come from," Tin-Puh said, chuckling without

humor, "guests do not to overrule the host when he shows them all wonders of the marvelous underground city."

This made the Wogglebug want to ask quite a number of questions, including, "how often does this situation come up?" And "Is this really a city?" and "if this is a city, where are all the citizens?" They had met plenty of foxes carving out walls but no one who appeared to actually live here. Before he could decide which question he should ask first, the Patchwork Girl yelled out "Ta-Da." And she raised herself to a handstand. Her dress flopped down while her legs wobbled making her look like a patchwork mushroom with a pair of un-mushroom-like fluttering stamen. She said, muffled by the batting of her skirt, "Where *do* you come from?"

The Wogglebug hoped that fear would give him strength. But he found his cold bug hands still not strong enough for winding a key. Scraps rolled herself from the floor and tried as well, but she only managed to braid her two arms together with one of her legs. She couldn't advance the copper gears by a single tooth as Tik-Tok nattered on and then stopped talking altogether.

She asked Tin-Puh again for help.

"There will be time, there will be time," said their host, freeing Scraps and rehanging the key. "He is still having thoughts and motions. And this is more than he is needing now."

Around the next corner, they came to yet another doorway, this one arched with an actual door in place. As Tin-Puh opened it, the artificial lights flickered and then went off.

"Happens," he said, pulling a flashlight from his belt, "be waiting here. I shall to get the lights to glow again."

The cone of Tin-Puh's marvelous hand-held artificial light floated away. It was all that could be seen in the muddy darkness. And then it disappeared and the darkness was absolute.

"Ooooooo," said the Patchwork Girl. "Doncha love it? Look, look, I can pluck my buttons right off my face and never see my fingers."

The Wogglebug didn't know what to say to that. His keen ears heard a faint snapping sound.

"Hmm," said the Patchwork Girl's voice, "better put these in my pocket. Probably need them later."

Tik-Tok started to shake, and his heavy feet came up and slammed down, rocking his heavy body back and forth with a crashing sound that echoed in the grand chamber.

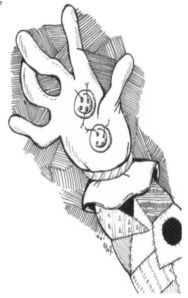

"Motion's going bye-bye," said Scraps.

The Wogglebug wanted to get his delicate body out of the way, but he couldn't see where to go.

The familiar sound of the copper man's always-moving gears stopped. He went still as a statue.

"I do hope that Tin-Puh finds the magic by which these lights work soon," the professor muttered.

"Why would you want that?" asked the Patchwork girl.

Light flooded the room as though someone were listening.

"Phew," said the Wogglebug.

"Hmmm," said the Patchwork girl turning her head in his direction. "Spose we'll get to hang out in the dark for days and days? Won't that be something?"

"Where are your eyes, Patchwork Girl?"

"Oh," pulling her hands out of her pockets and opening her fists, she revealed the two buttons formerly attached to her face. She raised one and pointed it at Tik-Tok. "Say, what're we gonna do about him?" The clockwork man stood between them, silent, but for a faint hum coming from his head, and unmoving. "All he's got left is his thoughts and no way to get 'em out."

Nine

Elephants were ripping up the forest. They were wrapping their trunks around the strong limbs of large trees and tearing them off, pulling the way a dog pulls at a toy you hold in your hand. Samantha had been to construction sites before. There was always a loud and constant moan of machines in those places with a lot of banging mixed in with the smell of burnt fuel, and puffs of black smoke hooting out of exhaust pipes. This wasn't like that. There was silence everywhere and then CRACK. And then silence and then another CRACK from a different place. And then CRACK, CRACK, CRACK from all over. Some of these cracks were loud and some were very loud. She watched the limbs get yanked off at a long distance without sound and then the crack would come when the broken branch was already off the tree, always louder than expected. The fading echoes threaded through the forest. Silences, brief but total, followed. It reminded Samantha of popcorn kernels randomly exploding.

After the branches were stripped, other elephants pulled the huge trunks with ropes tied to harnesses wrapped around their bodies. The pulling and dragging raised a visible layer of dust knee high. The ropes were lashed to the elephants' chests by—by foxes. Foxes were running all over the place like mice on hills of grain. It looked like the foxes were in charge of the elephants, skittering around with ropes in their mouths, twisting them around tree trunks then slithering in circles around the elephants before delivering the ends to the elephant's trunks for the elephants to secure them to their chests. The foxes seemed to be yelling at the elephants to pull like slaves until the trees cracked, the limbs sometimes snapping off entirely, sometimes needing to be pulled away from the trunks like licorice. Branches, limbs, and trunks were all being pulled along the ground across the open field by the elephants, single file, like ants, toward the mountain that stood out strangely on the plain, the mountain with a door on the bottom and a castle on top. It was hard work even for elephants. Some walked with a noticeable limp. Everything smelled of dirt, and fire, and fox, and elephant. Thick and musty. Where the animals had already come through, large root holes speckled the landscape.

Sam finally had to admit it: she really was in another country, and that country was Oz, like that movie her mother thought she should love because she loved it. So Oz was real. But it wasn't the same. The world of Judy Garland and the Scarecrow and the guy in the lion costume—and, oh yeah, the Tin Man, it didn't look anything like this world. It must have been one of those "based on a true story" things that aren't really anything like what actually happened. Like Cowboys and Indians movies. So if this really was Oz, saying that it was didn't really tell her anything. It wasn't helpful at all. If she found red shoes, there certainly wouldn't be any reason to put them on.

Across the cleared field, the mountain looked like it was made out of stones, as though someone had just collected them and piled them by the millions, brown and grey, like they were going to smooth the edges someday into a pyramid but never got around to it. The castle on top was made of the same stone, a huge structure with many walls and turrets, making it so you almost didn't notice it was up there on that pile because it was almost just part of the same wobbly-looking collection of rocks. It must be where that Wicked Witch lived. Out of the top of the castle, black smoke rose. They were burning the trees. And that was good because out here it was getting cold. Sam rubbed her arms.

That castle had to be where the problem was. Those people that were dressed in yellow—Mister Farmer Simplit and Mistress Dairyma'am Plitsim were their names—the ones who gave her soup, they told her all they knew about this new thing that was going on in Oz, which wasn't much. They said some new witch had moved in to the old witch's castle. She called herself a sorceress and a lady, but she was really just another witch without any real powers. No one knew what she wanted yet. She had not said. The only thing the farmer and the dairyma'am knew about her they had learned from a fox that Farmer Simplit had caught running through his corn. The fox told Farmer Simplit that Dox VII, the king of the foxes, had invited the sorceress to Foxville to show off the riches of that fairyland. Lady Mumps was impressed and said she would take it. She had millions of elephants and there was nothing King Dox VII could do to stop her. But the king was clever. He told her there was a bigger and more wonderful fairyland to the east called Oz. His great great great great great great grandfather had been to Oz oh-so-many years ago. And the king offered to help the Sorceress Lady Mumps conquer Oz if he'd leave Foxville alone. Lady Mumps took to that like a turkey to a gobble.

"But who could tell how much of what the fox said was true?" Farmer Simplit concluded the story. "He is a fox after all. And you know foxes."

"They only tell the truth by accident or if it serves them," Dairyma'am Plitsam said, "and it rarely serves them."

Sam didn't actually know any foxes. But she had heard stories.

"I suspect," said the farmer, "that Dox VII only offered Oz because he knew the so-called sorceress would be destroyed with all her elephants when she tried to cross the deadly desert. But that didn't happen."

"Stay away from her, whatever you do," Dairyma'am Plitsam continued. "You need to get to the Emerald City, where the great and powerful Ozma will help you."

"Help me what?" Sam asked.

"Get home, of course."

But Sam was in no hurry to get home. That Shaggy Man had told her what a wonderful place Oz was and how everyone was always happy and no one needed money and everyone did only the work they wanted to do and no one had to go to school if they didn't want to. Sam explained this to the farmer and his wife.

"Well, then," said Farmer Simplit, "you did not come at the right time. If that 'sorceress' gets her way, all that is lovely about Oz will vanish."

"Yes, you need to get to Ozma soon, because certainly the Sorceress Mumps is up to no good. Oz has been conquered before, you know. You need to get home while you still can."

"Unless you were brought here to save us," said Dairyma'am Plitsam.

"She's just a girl," said Farmer Simplit.

"We've been saved by 'just a girl' before. That's the best sort of savior there is. But maybe you should get home after all. We would never ask you to endanger yourself for us."

It seemed to Sam from what little she recalled of that dumb movie she'd watched that that was exactly the sort of thing Oz would ask her to do. But she didn't bring it up. What she said was, "But you don't really know what this Lady Mumps really wants, right?"

They had to admit that they didn't. And they also let on that Sam couldn't stay in Oz unless Ozma gave her permission. "We don't let just anyone into Oz," they said.

Sam had been wondering about Ozma and Lady Mumps and Oz all day, ever since she left the quaint home of the Dairyma'am and her husband. If that was the home they had and this castle was the home of the sorceress, then maybe you were better off being the sorceress than the quaint and humble farmer or dairyma'am. And if there was going to be a struggle for control of Oz, you were better off if you were on the winning side. You could try to stay neutral and then join up with whoever won afterwards, but that would only get you at most a humble little wooden igloo house and a few acres of corn. But if you were actually on the winning side and helped them win, then you'd really have something when the war was over. And if this Sorceress Mumps really was powerful (because they must be wrong about her having no powers of her own) and really was trying to take over Oz, then maybe she was best off joining up with her, that way she wouldn't have to worry about getting permission. And anyway, Oz would probably be more fun to be in charge of than just another person in.

But how could she get herself introduced to the sorceress? And what did she have to offer her? She'd have to sneak up the mountain past all the watchful foxes and elephants and trick her way past the guards into the warm castle and surprise this Mumps. And if she could do that, she'd show Mumps she needed better protection, and at the same time she'd show she had something to offer—her wits.

Sam crept along the edge of the cleared space, staying carefully hidden by the last row of standing trees, looking for an unguarded road.

Ten

Being careful didn't mean not talking to Winkies. True Winkies in the igloos were not likely to be dangerous, Louise assured Mildred and Thaddeus, who decided they had to believe her because it was dark out and cold, and invisible snowflakes were melting on their cheeks. They knocked on every door they saw, guided by the yellow glow of a fire in the little windows. But even with the help of the Love Magnet, the children found no one who would take them in. Every time the scene played out pretty much the same way. A small woman or man all dressed in yellow—whether young, a little older, or wrinkled from crown to chin—swung open the door with a smile and listened to the children's story. And as they listened, the smile decayed. By the time the story was through, the smile had become a hard frown. And it didn't matter who told the story, Thaddeus or Louise or even Mildred—who had to try because she was the one who actually had the Love Magnet in her pocket. They were always met with the same response.

"We're cold," one of the kids would say.

"This is Oz," they would say back. "You won't freeze to death." Then a firmly closed door and, on two occasions, a tightly pulled window shade.

"This is supposed to be freakin' Oz," said Louise. "The happiest place on earth."

"I thought that was Denmark," said Thaddeus.

"Even happier than Denmark," said Louise. "And we have the Love Magnet."

"I say we get rid of it," said Thaddeus. "It doesn't work."

"Then how would we get home?" said Mildred.

"I already answered that," said Louise, "and also, it could be working. We don't know it isn't working."

"What doors have *you* been knocking on?" said Thaddeus.

"Maybe they're just really scared of that Mumps. And we don't know how these people would have reacted if we *didn't* have the Love Magnet. Maybe they'd be even meaner."

"Like how? Like coming after us with clubs or something?" said Thaddeus.

"Anyway, as you both said, I'm the only one with the Love Magnet, so it should work better for me. But it's not any different."

"Well, not necessarily," said Thaddeus. "I mean I'm not saying it's doing anything but getting our hopes up, but real magnets don't work that way. They create these magnetic fields. The stronger the magnet is the bigger its field."

"Oh, said Louise, "that explains what happened in the river."

"No, it doesn't, said Thaddeus, "because it doesn't work. It doesn't actually *do* anything. I was just saying 'if it did.'"

"It's not good at making people love us," said Mildred.

"So there must be a *very* strong anti-magic coming from this Mumps or something," said Louise. "It's a good thing we have the Love Magnet or no telling what would happen."

"We can test that," said Thaddeus. "Let's get rid of it."

Louise's eyes shot open wide, "No."

"We can't. We're going to need it to get home," Mildred said. She was getting tired of having to make the same point over and over.

"Not neces*sar*ily," said Louise, who was growing tired of giving the same response. "But we still can't get rid of it."

"Even if *pos*sibly," said Mildred. "You don't throw away your bus ticket because you're hoping a stranger in a limo might come by."

Thaddeus wasn't sure that was the right way to think about it.

The rising moon shed a dim light on the large, lightly falling flakes of snow when they knocked on the next door. A smiling young Winkie with a candle opened her door eagerly. A sense of defeat settled on the three children at the sight of the smile.

"Why so glum?" said the woman, as her smile started to fade.

Mildred decided not to ask if she could offer a warm place to sleep for the night. Instead she asked, "I thought Oz was kind to strangers. Why is everyone around here so mean?"

"You're strangers?" said the woman, taking a step back and putting her hand on the door as though she were preparing to slam it shut at a moment's notice.

"We are," said Thaddeus.

"I see by your clothes that you are."

"But we're nice," said Mildred, wiping her cheek.

"I'm sure you are." The woman's voice trembled a little. And she opened the door a little wider as though she were going to invite them in. But as soon as she made room for them to pass, she pushed the door again leaving just a little space for her to see and talk through. "Tell the sorceress we do not want her here." The nervous tremble grew in her voice. "Tell her her kind of magic is forbidden in Oz. Tell her the Princess Ozma will not tolerate what she is doing in that castle."

"The Sorceress Mumps? We don't know her. We're not with her."

The woman straightened up and opened the door a little wider, not wide enough for anyone to pass through but wide enough to stand in. And then she took a breath and closed it a little. "But that's what you'd say if you did and you were. Tell her to take her birds and her elephants and her foxes and go back where she came from. Tell her to leave the forest alone."

"But we need…" said Mildred.

"I'm sorry, I don't have any," said the woman. And she closed the door and slid a bolt loud enough for them to hear.

"Well, that's it," said Louise.

"That's what?" said Mildred.

"What's it?" said Thaddeus.

"You're right. They're all afraid of this Sorceress Mumps. And they think we're with her because we're not from here. You can see why the Love Magnet is not strong enough to overcome *that*."

"But we still need a place to stay for the night," said Mildred.

Although they were not as cold as they thought they should be, snow was falling pretty thickly.

"Barn's unlocked," came a trembly voice through the door.

Thaddeus was afraid the woman would call in a posse of Winkie farmers to capture them. But Louise and Mildred, lightly shivering, decided they had no choice, and all three of them spent their first night in Oz covered in hay in a Winkie barn.

Eleven

"It's a good thing I brought these food pills," the Wogglebug said, popping one in his mouth and straining to swallow it. Tin-Puh had not returned since they'd been caught behind these bars, and no one had thought to bring food or drink to the flesh-and-blood member of the traveling party.

"But I would like a drink of water," he said.

"Should have brought some water pills," said the Patchwork Girl. She was holding one of her button eyes in her hand so she could see. The other one was in her pocket.

"You can't fit much water in a capsule."

"Unless you have a big one," Scraps threw her arms out until they wound and unwound behind her back.

"But you see," the Wogglebug began his response.

"Ball me up," said the Patchwork Girl. She was already bored with the conversation about the pills. "Don't know why you need to water yourself anyway. You're not a flower. Ball me up." She placed her hands behind her neck and folded herself in half. The Wogglebug saw what she was about.

Changing strategy, Scraps laid herself flat on the floor and tried rolling her hand up into her arm. But that wasn't the way she was used to moving, and it wasn't easy to do. The Wogglebug had a little more success rolling his companion into the shape of a tube which was compact enough to push through the bars.

"Hey, what'd you do that for?" she said when she unrolled herself on the other side of the bars. "Don'tcha like me?" She raised her arm and moved it all around to get as many angles of sight as she could. "Everyone should have eyes on the ends of their fingers."

"Wasn't that the point? Escape, I mean."

"Nah. I just wanted to know what it was like to be a ball. I suppose I could escape. Want me to find you some water?"

"I'd settle for a key." The Wogglebug rattled the door.

"Can't drink a key," said Scraps. "You can be very silly. You know that?" And off she scurried, leaving the Wogglebug wondering whether he'd made a wise choice in helping her through the bars.

"Done is done," he muttered, putting one tentacle arm on Tik-Tok, who was standing still, in the middle of the cell, like a statue. Then he sat down and pulled a book out of one of the large pockets of his oversized dress jacket and, now that there was a moment of peace and quiet for the first time since this tiresome trip had begun, he began to read.

He had not completed a single chapter of *The Absurd Tale of the Burzee Rose* when, from the dark, far reaches of whatever room lay in front of the cell, Scraps returned, on the back of the Cowardly Lion, with the head of the Tin Man in her arms.

Twelve

The invasion of the castle didn't go exactly as Sam had hoped.

Unable to find an unguarded road, and, growing hungry and cold, she slipped in among the foxes as they were guiding their elephants to stables carved out of the base of the castle mountain. She used the trick she'd learned (if you can call something "learned" that comes to you as naturally as leaves come to a tree)—the trick that she'd *picked up* from her father on the day she joined a youth softball team even though the sign ups and tryouts were over and the season was about to start. That day, she just walked out onto the field and joined the practice as though she were already a member of the team. It was a long time before anyone said anything, and by the time they did, she'd figured out what they wanted to hear, and that's what she told them. And the next thing she knew, she was on the team. Her father came down to the field to pick her up.

"I see you've learned my trick," he said.

"Yes, I guess I have," she said back, although she had no idea what he was talking about.

"Act confident, pretend you know what you're doing, pretend you are where you belong, and most people will believe you are. And if not, they'll be much too shy to say anything about it. You can't believe how many doors that has opened for me."

"Act confident," she repeated.

"Absolutely," he chuckled. "If you figure out how to *act* confident, then you don't even have to *be* confident. That speeds things along just fine. No difference, really."

As soon as she'd heard him say that, she knew that that had always been her strategy, and it would always be her strategy because it worked so well. Most people are so shy and have so little self-confidence that if you act as though you are where you belong, they'll doubt their own doubt. It worked with foxes too, at first.

She hadn't said anything. She'd just walked up to the foxes, many of whom wore clothes and walked on two legs, and she grabbed a long stick she'd found on the ground just to have something in her hand that seemed to give her a purpose, and she marched right along with them wherever they were going.

One or two foxes gave her a funny look, and one, wearing a crown, looked down from the elephant he was riding and seemed about to speak.

"Don't worry," she called up, "we got that last stump out that that elephant tripped over. I think he'll be fine, by the way. Excellent strategy you suggested." Then she looked at the young fox walking beside her and said loud enough for the crowned one on the elephant to hear, "We're lucky to have such a wise and experienced leader or we'd take another month finishing this job."

The fox on the elephant didn't say whatever it was he had been going to say.

Things went a little less smoothly when Samantha entered the castle. Trying to figure out a plan to meet up with the Sorceress Mumps, she'd proceeded along with a bevy of scurrying foxes through a maze of snaky hallways in the mountain and up several floors in the castle to a great big, crumbling hall where they all sat at tables, and where other foxes served everyone plates of barely edible food—raw vegetables and piles of eggs that had been hardboiled and mashed, and some undercooked thing that she guessed was a tiny chicken. Hungry as she was, she ate it all pretty quickly. Still, before she'd quite finished her meal, the fox that wore the crown rushed into the hall, pointing and talking. Next thing she knew two foxes were poking her with the handles of swords and ordering her to get up.

She did not act scared. She didn't really feel scared, just surprised.

"Not finished my food yet," she said.

"Tut, tut," said one of the foxes to the other.

"Tsk, tsk," returned the other to the one.

And all the foxes at the long table looked up from their plates and swiveled their heads and stared at her.

"Just about done," she said. She was sure she could scare these two foxes off with one or two swift kicks. But she didn't do that. For one thing, she noticed that every other fox at the table also had a sword, and one had a sword and an ax, and she was not sure she had that many kicks in her. But more than that, she didn't think she'd make a good impression on the Sorceress Mumps if she maimed all her foxes.

Saying nothing more than "move along," they led her up more flights of stairs to an abandoned, roofless room where they locked her up. No one brought her any more food.

The night was long and cold. And at one point it started to snow. But she buried herself in a pile of hay or straw to keep as warm as she could, and the snow stopped soon after it started, and she eventually got so tired with nothing to do but stare up at the clouds blowing across the stars that she managed to fall asleep. She awoke the next morning to the noisy sound of countless hungry birds pouring out from what must have been the room below the one she was in. They rose like a cloud, like a narrow stream of water from a hose that expanded as soon as it was released. As the room had no roof, it was easy to watch the birds scream up in a cloud of green smoke and fill the sky. The smoke filled the room with an odor like sulfur, and the noise from the flapping of thousands of wings doubled the noise of the continuous and barely modulating screech from their collective lungs. The taunting screech and the slap of their wings against the hollow of their chests went on for minute on minute. It was a long time before the sky was blue again, and Sam exhaled and took her hands off her ears.

Her ears hurt. But she was smiling too, to see so much force, so much energy. It was like nothing she'd ever seen before, nothing like the little grey birds that hopped around her mother's bird feeder, taking turns at the little seeds, always afraid of everything.

But then they were gone. And the sky was blue with puffy clouds, and the air was wild with the smell of the birds, and the only sound was the ringing in her ears.

She was in a cold, damp room high up in the castle, a prisoner. Her plan to impress the sorceress had not worked—yet. But she was confident she could fix things. She wasn't afraid. She decided she could escape at any time she wanted to, although she wasn't exactly sure how she would do that. But these captors just didn't seem all that bright. They'd be pretty easy to fool. There wasn't much in the room, just this pile of grass or hay or straw that she'd slept in. And there was a little table. There were three good walls—interior castle walls—and one outside wall that was starting to crumble just at the top. It had a steel ring attached to it. And there was a barrel and some metal cans or tubes the purpose of which was not obvious. Some unused drain pipe maybe. The room hadn't had a ceiling in a while judging from the water stains on all the walls and on how far away the next bit of sound roof was. Fluffy marshmallow clouds meandered through the cold sky.

She noticed the corner of a piece of blue cloth sticking out from the hay—a shirt or jacket, patched and thin, useless but for spreading on the hay and sitting on.

Lowering herself onto it, she cried out immediately, but not very loud, from a sharp poke on her leg. She reached back to find a pin, a common pin, sticking out of her thigh.

Well, look at that, she thought, *like a needle in a haystack,* though it was really a common pin, and this wasn't necessarily hay. Maybe it was straw. But still, maybe it was a sign of good luck.

She tossed the pin aside.

It landed on another piece of blue cloth—that turned out to be a pair of patched, blue pants. How odd.

If she really wanted to escape quickly, she could climb on the table, tie the pants to the steel ring and then tie the shirt to the pants to make a rope and use it to hop over the wall, if the fall on the other side wasn't too great.

But it probably was. And that wasn't what she wanted to do anyway. She needed a plan to find the sorceress. Perhaps she could yell and make a stink until they opened the door and then overpower whoever came in and just make a break for it. But they did have swords. And who knew how the sorceress would react to that sort of a jailbreak. It didn't seem like a very clever way to get out. She could try to outsmart the foxes and give them an excuse to bring her to the sorceress. But how would she do that? She sat on the floor and put her back against the wall. "Hmmm," she said.

"Hmmm," the sound seemed to echo from under the barrel lying beside her. How odd. She kicked it.

It rolled; it rolled much farther than it should have from the force of her kick.

Underneath it was a flat piece of cloth with a face painted on it.

"Hmmm?" said the face.

"What the…" Samantha picked up the cloth to see what was under it.

"I sure hope you've come to rescue us," said the cloth face.

Samantha almost dropped it. For just a moment she felt a twinge of fear—an emotion very strange to her. But it passed, and she turned over the cloth.

"Woah," said the cloth. "Turn me back."

"What is this?"

"It's a head. My head. Or it would be if it had any stuffing in it. Right now I guess it's just a face. Pleased to meet you," it said. "I'm the Scarecrow."

"You don't look like a scarecrow."

"True, at the moment I'm not *a* scarecrow, but still I am *the* Scarecrow. And I will be a scarecrow again if you'd be kind enough to stuff my head and reattach it to my body."

Samantha turned the cloth around again to see if there was perhaps a microphone or something taped on the back side of it.

"Oh, dear," said the cloth. "Is that the Tin Woodman? Where is his head?"

"This is weird." Samantha turned the cloth back around.

"Hey, hey, little dizzy," the cloth said. "Keep me still and I'll tell you what happened."

The cloth seemed to be on the verge of launching into a story that Samantha saw no reason to hear. "If I put you together, can you get me out of here?" she said.

"I will need brains to answer that question," said the cloth. "Look for a mess of pins."

"Pins?" she said the word as though it was the unlikely answer to a riddle she'd been thinking of for a long time. She pushed aside the hay she'd sat on—and there, where her leg had been, was a whole pile of pins—about two handfuls. "I could have been stuck like a porcupine," she said.

"You mean *by* a porcupine, I think," said the cloth.

Just then the big barrel rolled over without being pushed and some of the small tubes jerked around a little as well like the plucked appendages of a daddy longlegs.

"What was that?" Samantha said.

"That's the Tin Woodman's body. But where is the head?"

"How many heads are in this cell?" said Samantha.

"Two that we know of. If you collect my brain and put my body back together, we can look for more," the cloth face said.

Samantha dropped the cloth and started digging in the hay or straw or whatever it was.

"Of course," mumbled the cloth that was now wadded up on the floor, "your way may be good too. Until I have my brains back, I don't want to say."

Samantha kept looking.

"Of course, I have no idea how we'll get the Tin Woodman out if we don't find his head. Even if we put him back together, how will we tell him to walk? I hope my brains can puzzle that one out," the cloth said.

But Samantha did not find a tin head anywhere. She did find a pair of gloves, two boots, a hat, and some short pieces of rope. She picked up the cloth face and stuffed it with bedding and then dropped the pins in and only pricked her hand twice. She tied the sack off with one of the pieces of rope.

"I have an idea," said the head as soon as it was tied off. "Show me the Tin Woodman's body."

Samantha turned the head in the direction of the barrel.

"Yes, I was right. There are several holes where the arms and the legs and the head go. Fill the body with straw, then stuff my body inside and then put my head on top. Then we can go out together.

This was not hard to do. Sam stuffed a tin armhole with straw (the Scarecrow head told her it was all straw) until the barrel was pretty full. She rolled up the jacket and the pants and the gloves and stuffed them into a hollow leg. She managed with some squeezing to get the boots onto the barrel through one of the leg holes. Then she put all the pieces together as the head directed. It was actually kind of fun. She had never been one for solving puzzles, but this one was pretty easy now that she knew what the pieces represented.

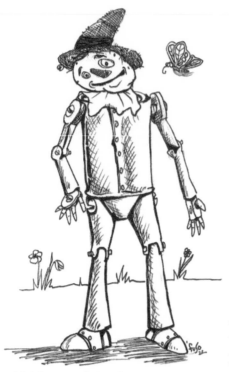

They went together with ingenious little bits of metal that the Scarecrow told her were called "cotter pins" ("ingenious, perhaps, but not good for brains," he said). These had been taken out carefully and left in a heap in one of the tin feet. When the arms and legs were all successfully pinned to the body, she stuck the head onto a little stem that stuck up on the top of the drum. The full-grown Tin Woodman's body was taller than she was, and he or it looked very strange with the sagging, cloth Scarecrow head on top. But then it would probably look pretty strange with any head on top.

The secure tin arms rose and grabbed and adjusted the two sides of the head and put the wide-brimmed blue hat on top.

"Oh, yes, that's good," said the head.

But then immediately the hands shot down and the legs started to move.

"Oh, dear," said the head. "I'm not doing that."

The body took two large steps and crashed chest first into the wall of the cell.

"Stop that," the head said.

"You're weird," Sam said.

The Scarecrow-headed Tin Woodman spun around and headed across the room. "No, no. I think I—" It slowed down. "Wait." It spun half-way toward the door and went up on one leg. It looked as though it was going to fall over.

"What are you doing?" Sam asked.

"I believe wherever it is, the Tin Woodman's head is struggling with my head for control of this body.

"Well this won't work if you can't stand still," said Sam.

Then the clanging stopped. And the Scarecrow Man said, "I think he's stopped." Sam turned to see the arms moving in a controlled motion. The legs and barrel did a little happy dance. "Yes, he has. I have full control."

"Good. Come here," Sam said.

And the Scarecrow Man tap danced over. She stood beside the door, climbed on top of the barrel, and stuck a foot on the back of his head, which set her just high enough to pull herself up into the top of the wall.

"What are you doing?" the Scarecrow Man asked.

"Why else would I put you together?" she said. "I needed something to step on." She pulled herself higher and slithered over the wall and dropped onto the floor of the hall and ran away.

Thirteen

Even after all the trouble they'd had, Mildred and Louise and Thaddeus all slept pretty well. When they awoke, the sun was high and they were hungry. Opening the door to the barn, they found a tray lying atop a layer of snow so thin, the weight of the tray had melted a green rectangle. Footsteps of grass made a path to the little house that almost invited them to follow it. On the tray was a bowl filled with hard-boiled eggs and beside the bowl a tall stack of buttered bread. There was also a pitcher of water and a note.

> *Tell the Sorceress Ozma will forget the harm she's done and*
> *give her free passage wherever she came from if she promises*
> *to leave. Enjoy your breakfast. Then go away.*

"That's kind of a weird note," said Thaddeus.

As they ate, the sky darkened again as it had the day before. Far off, over trees in the direction of the mountain, a dark cloud rose like black fire from a vast chimney. It swirled like chocolate in a glass of milk, and then it whirled out in all directions. In no time, the screaming river of birds was coursing overhead, so much closer now, even lower in the sky, that the friends could make out individual birds in the black mass with dots and pools of blue and white. As the smoke got closer, it turned, or seemed to turn, green.

Thaddeus took his fingers off his ears and pointed up, holding a hard-boiled egg in his pointing hand. "What are they doing?" he asked. But the birds were too loud for Louise or Mildred to hear what Thaddeus was saying.

Three birds fell out of the cloud while Thaddeus' hand was still in the air, two black, one blue. They didn't dive like hawks, they fell more like water balloons, puffy fat birds. They seemed to fold their wings in and drop out of the sky. Thaddeus lowered his hand. More birds dropped. Faster and faster they fell. The children ducked as the birds spread their wings and landed not two feet from the remainder of breakfast. The thick cloud of birds coursed over their heads. More and more fell out of formation and dropped toward the children. The ones on the ground twittered horrible sounds as they charged at the food with sharp beaks open wide.

Thaddeus cowered. Mildred drew her food close to her body to protect it. Louise got up and charged at the birds. She'd never known a bird that wasn't afraid of a charging human. Not even a seagull. But these birds were not afraid of anything. And more were landing in big plops like sacks of cement. A big blue one snapped at Louise. Thaddeus just watched.

"They're after our breakfast," he yelled.

"They're after us," Louise yelled back.

"Into the barn," Mildred yelled. And the three of them abandoned their breakfast and bolted the door behind them.

By now there were maybe two dozen birds on the ground with big, dead eyes and large snapping beaks. They gobbled up the uneaten food, then they charged at the door to the barn and shook it like a hard wind. When it wouldn't give, they shook it some more. On all sides, they knocked against the barn walls like hail. They forced their beaks into the knotholes and the spaces between the vertical boards of the walls. The children, watching, jumped back and screeched. And then, failing to get in, the birds left, flew off suddenly and all at once. The screeching died down. The children saw it all.

When they walked out of the barn, the sky was clear again and blue and the cloud of birds was a faraway chatter. The air was colder than before.

"It's very hard to get a whole meal in this place," said Mildred.

"Are you sure this Oz is safe?" Thaddeus asked Louise. "Those birds were trying to attack us."

"They were just trying to get food," Mildred said.

"If they'd got into the barn…"

"They would have seen there was no food and left," Louise said.

"You don't know that," Thaddeus said. "I don't think it's safe."

"It's almost always safe in the books," she said.

"Almost?"

"Not if you were a wicked witch, of course. I'm not worried," she said.

Thaddeus looked miffed.

"Doesn't matter. Just be careful," said Mildred.

"And the Shaggy man said we wouldn't get hurt, didn't he?"

"Doesn't matter," Mildred repeated. "When there's only one road, you have to take it." She stooped down to collect the scattered plates.

"Just leave them," said Thaddeus. "It's not like she was that nice to us."

"She gave us breakfast,"

"Yeah, but…"

"If you're a little nicer to people than they are to you, they might learn to be nicer the next time."

Thaddeus rolled his eyes, but he helped Mildred and Louise gather the plates and put them on the tray and take them to the welcome mat of the little cottage. Mildred said they needed to thank the woman.

They knocked and they waited. The sound of shuffling, like old slippered feet, approached the door, paused, then went away. They left the tray on the mat and headed off.

Mildred pulled out the Love Magnet and held it. "Some Love Magnet," she said. She still thought she probably needed it to get back home, despite what Louise had said, but her real desire was just to drop it and step on it and walk away.

"I'll carry it," said Thaddeus.

Mildred rested it on the flat of her hand. She felt a sensation like a small animal, like a mouse twisting in her hand. The magnet shifted around, all on its own, like the needle of a compass moving to find the north pole. It tickled. The magnet turned its tines in the direction of the sunrise.

"That's not north," said Mildred.

"Horseshoe magnets don't point north," said Thaddeus, drawing the horseshoe shape in the air.

The magnet hopped out of Mildred's hand and raced across the ground like a cat after a chipmunk. Then it picked up speed. Thaddeus took off after it, and, after several attempts to reach down and pick it up, he stomped on it. He held it under his shoe like a curling snake. Louise picked it up.

"It's like it has a mind of its own."

"Maybe it only makes people love you when it wants to," said Mildred.

It continued to pull, but not with great force, like a small child with a hand on your pantleg.

"Should we follow it?" said Mildred.

Thaddeus laid it back on the ground—and off it flew.

"I didn't mean let it go."

But it was too late. They all three ran after the fleeing magnet. It skipped over the ground like a flat stone across a pond. It kicked up a flurry of dust and small rocks that flew up into the children's eyes and faces. The dirt felt like little pins or like the icy rain that sometimes blows in your face on cold winter days. It made the magnet hard to follow. But they kept at it. Over flat ground, into a patch of trees where the magnet hit a root and jumped up and bounced off the trunk of a tree. It moved like something attached to a string reeled in by a motor. They could barely keep up with it. They couldn't talk. They couldn't look at each other. Mildred ran short of breath. She fell behind. Then the same thing happened to Thaddeus. Only Louise was able to keep pace with the magnet, but she wasn't gaining.

Thaddeus was the first to stop, huffing to catch his breath. Mildred came up to him at a slow jog. "C'mon it's getting away," she said.

"Slow down," he called to her. "We'll never catch it."

That was true, of course, she realized. Either Louise would catch it or it would get away. There was no point in running any more.

"How does a magnet do that?" Thaddeus asked.

"I guess anything can happen in Oz." Mildred pulled in shallow breaths.

"I wish there were rules," Thaddeus said. "It's very confusing not to know what is and isn't possible."

Louise was out of sight by then. But the trail was clearly marked by little magnet scars on the ground. Anyway, it had been going in a pretty straight line all the while. So they weren't too worried about getting lost.

"Even if we do find it, do we know where we're going with it?" Thaddeus asked.

"If we do what the note says, we have to deliver a message to the Sorceress Mumps."

"Why should we do what the note says?"

"She gave us breakfast," said Mildred.

"She made us sleep in a barn," said Thaddeus.

Up ahead, the magnet charged through the underbrush at a steady pace. Louise however was starting to run out of steam. She didn't have to look around to know the other two were no longer with her. It was up to her to save them. But she didn't think she could do it unless it ran into a rock and got confused—something it would have to do very soon, before she collapsed.

Louise kept her eyes glued to the running, skipping, fleeing magnet. Up ahead a form appeared, a little man wearing a hat that reflected the sun into her eyes. She tripped. She fell forward, flat on the rough ground. She groaned. She felt a dull pain in the palms of her hands as though she'd been slapped by a stick. Her friends, too far behind to see her, heard her call out and broke again into a run. The little man in front of her must have heard her too, he was so close. But he didn't even turn his head. Lying on the ground, Louise watched the magnet jump a little root and skip toward the little man—his boots were as shiny as his hat. He stepped on the magnet as though it were a small animal or a bug he wanted to crush. He picked it up and turned it over. Then he stuck the magnet to his funnel-topped hat like a handle.

"Excuse me," Louise panted. "Hi. That's my…mine." She pointed to the magnet.

The little man in the metal hat turned toward her but didn't say anything.

"Could I please have it back."

"What business are you having in the Mumpslands?" the man asked.

"I... we, we don't have any... we just want to find our way home." She was just starting to get her breath back.

"We?" said the man. Just then Mildred and Thaddeus arrived, panting.

"He has the magnet," Louise said.

"He also has a hatchet," said Thaddeus. Louise hadn't noticed that. The man held a small silver-colored hatchet.

"Indeed, I do," the little man said. "Home is not being in this direction."

"We need the magnet to get home," Mildred said. "After that, you're welcome to it."

The little man pulled it off his head and stared at it. "I am seeing," he said, apparently to himself. Then he raised his eyes to the children, re-attached the magnet to his hat and moved the hatchet from his left hand to his right as he said again, "Home is not being in this direction." And he turned away from them and started off toward the castle on the mountain.

"We can take it back. It's ours," said Louise.

"He's a grown-up," said Thaddeus.

"But he's not much bigger than we are," said Mildred.

"He has a hatchet," said Thaddeus.

He was already nearly out sight through the heavy foliage. The children took a step forward. And then they caught sight of something else moving through the trees. It was a woman, and when they heard her voice call out to the man and saw the red of her dress among the leaves, they knew it was the Witch Lloco-Monnem. And they decided they didn't like the odds.

Fourteen

They greeted each other warmly: the Lion and the Tin Woodman's head greeted the Wogglebug, and Tik-Tok, and the Wogglebug greeted the Cowardly Lion and the Tin Head. The Patchwork Girl ended the merry meeting by greeting everyone, those she brought with her and those she'd so recently left. She did this not because she'd forgotten where she was or who she was with (even though her eyes were in her pocket and she could not see a thing) but because greeting old friends is so much fun. The last on her list was the copper-bellied clockwork man.

"I see you're not very friendly today," said the Tin Woodman's head to the clockwork man.

"Perhaps he's afraid someone will hear us," said the Lion.

"Yeah, but he's already in a cage," said Scraps, "so what's he afraid of, really?"

"Motion stopped," said the Wogglebug.

"Oh, right," said the Patchwork Girl, "also can't talk."

"At least he can think," said the Tin Head, which was fortunately pointing in the direction of the Clockwork Man.

"He can?" said Scraps.

"Just listen. There's a hum coming from his head."

And everyone went quiet and heard the hum. It was a steady, low hum like the sound of a fan that you know is there only if the room gets really quiet or if someone happens to mention it.

"If only he could think his way out of the cage," said Scraps.

"I don't suppose you brought a key," said the Wogglebug.

"I brought a lion and a talking Tin Head," said Scraps. "Can't get everything."

"By the way, why are you just a head?" the Wogglebug asked.

"Too bad Tik-Tok's key won't fit the lock," Scraps said because she'd already heard the Tin Man's story and didn't want to hear it again.

"You know it just might at that," the Wogglebug said. "Don't know why it didn't occur to me before. Must be the cold. All the keys and locks in Oz are made at my college."

"Oh?" said the lion.

"And we only make one size. It seemed absurd to make several, there being no crime to speak of in Oz."

"You're saying the same key fits all locks?" the Patchwork Girl asked. "And no one ever noticed?"

"Well, why would they? Every lock comes with its own key. They'd have to put the wrong key in the wrong lock on purpose for that to happen. And that would not be honest."

"But what if they did it by mistake?" Scraps asked.

"Well then they did it thinking it was the right key, and the results would be the same. No, no, no. Honest people only need one kind of key."

"As long as they have a lot of 'em," said Scraps.

The Patchwork Girl felt for the hole in the door lock and slid the Tik-Tok key in. It was exactly the right size. "Well, I'll be," said Scraps. All they had to do then was turn it and it would unlock the door. But they ran into the same trouble they'd had when the Clockwork Man ran down: there was not a hand among them capable of turning the key. Not even the lion could do it. His paws were strong and his claws were versatile, but they were not fine enough to turn a small key in a little lock.

The humming sound of Tik-Tok's mechanical brain whirred on. As the conversation about the key grew and fell, the sound of Tik-Tok's brain got faster and higher in pitch, until it was no longer like a background noise of a fan but more like a mosquito right in the porches of your ear.

"I think he wants to say something," said Scraps, pointing the Tin Head in the direction of the sound as though she could see through his eyes. "Maybe we should wind him."

"But we can't," said the Wogglebug. "It's a double bind. If we could wind him we could open the lock and if we could open the lock, we could wind him."

"Wonder what he's trying to tell us," said Scraps.

"He must have a solution to the problem," said the Tin Head.

"And that means there *is* a solution to the problem," said the Lion, scratching his head.

Everyone stared at Tik-Tok as though staring would release his imprisoned thoughts. The hum grew louder and higher.

"Oh, he must really be thinking up a storm," said Scraps. "I hope he doesn't melt."

And then suddenly the humming became very high and very fast and then, suddenly, it stopped altogether.

"Well, now we'll never know," said Scraps.

"I don't see how we were going to know in any case," said the Lion.

And then everyone looked at everyone else, one at a time, for several seconds.

"I have it," said the Wogglebug.

"Well give it to us," said Scraps, flipping a button eye like a coin and trying to catch it.

And he told the Patchwork Girl to put the key in the Tin Head's mouth. And he told the Tin Head to bite down hard. And the he told the Lion to turn the head. His paws were plenty precise enough for that.

The lion stood on his hind feet and put a forepaw on the Tin Man's eye. And he put the other forepaw on the Tin Man's jaw. The Tin Head bit down hard on the handle of the key. And the key turned as easily as a fork in a plate of spaghetti.

With one echoing click, the door was open. They tried the same key-turning system on Tik-Tok as well, and he was rocking back and forth in what could easily be mistaken for glee in no time. With just a little difficulty, the Lion's paws and the Tin Woodman's mouth wound the clockwork tight for motion and thoughts and speech. They found his thoughts a little warm at first, but in a short time, everything was back to normal.

"We didn't bend your mouth funny, did we, Tin Man?" the Wogglebug asked.

"Nothing a ball peen hammer won't easily mend," the Tin Head said with a very slight lisp.

"Must be hard not to have a body," said Scraps.

"Oh, I have a body," said the Tin Head. "It's just not here."

"But it's not one you can move," said Scraps.

"Oh, but I think I can," said the Tin Head. "I've been trying to move it all day, and I feel as though I'm having some success. Why just a little while ago…"

"Well not one that can move you," the Patchwork Girl jumped in so that he wouldn't tell his unhappy story again.

"Where do we go now?" asked the Wogglebug.

"WE are on a MIS-sion from OZ-MA to the BROK-en CAST-LE."

"Oh, but they've already been there." Scraps waved her arms to indicate the Lion and the Tin Head. "Not a fun place."

"STILL," said Tik-Tok, "that IS WHERE WE are go-ING."

"Shall we think this through and take a vote?" asked the Wogglebug.

"you CAN," said the Grand Army of Oz, "BUT WE are go-ING to the CAST-le."

"Oh, right. He's the leader. Said so himself. So off we go," said Scraps. And then she pulled a sheet of paper from her pocket. "In that case, we may need this."

It was the map Tin-Puh had shown them.

"But we don't need a map to find our way in Oz," said the Tin Head.

"BUT i WOULD LIKE to see IT." Tik-Tok looked over the map. Although he had not said anything when he had been shown them before, he thought there was something odd about it. "Ah," he said. "this is WHY I am PUZzled." And he pointed at the spot representing the castle. "HERE with a BIG X through IT it SAYS 'cap-i-TAL.'"

The Wogglebug held the map to his many-faceted eyes. "But that's the castle of the Wicked Witch."

"I always thought the Emerald City was the capital," said Scraps. "Learn something new every day."

"But it is. Why would they call *that* the capital?" the Tin Head asked.

No one could explain it until the professor decided it showed that Tin-Puh was indeed an outsider with a very slight knowledge of Oz. "It was an error on his map. That's why the big X was through it."

And everyone seemed satisfied until Scraps said, "Unless the plan is to make a new capital."

"Ah, but you see…" said the Wogglebug.

"'fraid I don't," said Scraps "eyes in my deep, dark pocket. Let's find a way out."

As they combed the dim, salt-smelling tunnels of Tin-Puh's cavern, the Lion and the Tin Head filled the rest in on what they knew.

The Lion, the Tin Woodman, and the Scarecrow had indeed made it to the castle where they had been caught by a patrol of foxes and dragged before a huge little woman in a flowing pink gown who wore a gold-plated barrel hoop on her head and called herself the Sorceress Lady Mumps.

"Huge and little?" asked the Wogglebug.

"She was shaped kind of sideways," said the Tin Head. "Like a trunk. A long way from side to side but not so far from slipper to hoop."

"I'm getting kind of tired of lugging this mumbling head," said Scraps. "Anyone else want to give it try?"

"You can't get tired," said the Tin Head.

"Then I'm getting bored. These arms have got to be free." And at that she threw her arms up in the air and the Tin Woodman's head went up as well and turned over three times before the Wogglebug caught it.

"But I *can* get tired," said the Wogglebug. "And you have the best arms for carrying the Tin Head."

"Oh, all right," she said. "But he needs to get himself some legs and maybe a body, or at least mumble interesting things."

"Oh, I've been trying," said the Tin Head. "I don't know where my body is, but I can tell it's moving. If I could figure out where it was, I think I could get it to come to me."

"Tell US MORE aBOUT this SOR-cer-ESS," said Tik-Tok.

"She had a mane that made her seem taller than she was," the Lion told them.

"It was really a tall wig like cotton candy," the Tin Head added, "which, had it been actual cotton candy would have been pumpkin flavored."

The Scarecrow, the Lion, and the Tin Woodman had approached the Sorceress Mumps to find out what she was up to, as the Princess Ozma had ordered. But they'd hardly opened their mouths before the Lady Mumps said to the Tin Woodman, "My friend Tin-Puh is looking for you," and then to the Lion, "you will carry his head where I tell you to go," and then to the Scarecrow, "you must be disassembled and thrown in a cell along with the disassembled body of the Tin Can. If the Lion does not deliver the head to my friend Tin-Puh, I will have you burned up and I'll use him for the oven."

"My, my," said Scraps.

"She didn't," said the Wogglebug.

"Oh, but she did," said the Tin Head.

"She's not very nice," said the Lion.

"Then isn't that where your body is?" The Patchwork Girl asked.

"Probably," said the Tin Head, "but I don't know where in the castle that would be."

"I did what she said," the Lion cut in. "I brought the head to Tin-Puh who said he was very sad to see the head without a body. And then he tossed the head into the trash and said, "the part I want is the body."

"It turned out the sorceress just used my head as proof to Tin-Puh that she had the body," the Tin Head explained.

"That IS AW-ful," said Tik-Tok.

But it got worse.

"Just this morning before Tin-Puh left for the castle, a woman in a dirty red costume showed up in the tunnel carrying a hatful of dust," the Lion told them. "And she warned Tin-Puh of a gang of nasty children roaming Oz who might cause trouble."

"Whose side are these children on?" asked the Wogglebug.

"Are there sides?" asked the Patchwork Girl.

"Of course there are sides," said the Wogglebug. "There are always sides."

"Are these insides and outsides or north sides and south sides? Or are they left sides and right sides, or east sides and west sides?"

"They are good sides and bad sides," said the Wogglebug.

"If they are nasty children, they would have to be on the bad side," said Scraps.

"I think that is true," said the Tin Head.

"So which side are we on?" asked Scraps, but no one seemed to hear her.

"SO we WILL HAVE to LOOK out FOR THEM. A-VOID them."

They had come to the end of a long hallway by then, moving farther and farther from any light source. They could see that the hallway forked in front of them but they could not see down either fork more than a little ways.

"What do we do now?" asked the Wogglebug.

"What do we do about what?" asked the Patchwork Girl, whose eyes were still in her pocket.

"We've never been here," said the Tin Head.

"Oh, I have," said Scraps, and she climbed onto the back of the Lion. "I went everywhere looking for the key. Follow me."

Fifteen

The smell in the hallway stuck like pins up Sam's nose. She could only think that someone who ate a lot of hamburgers had forgot to flush the toilet. She tried to breathe shallow and ignore it.

She had to avoid being captured again. She saw no guards. What did that mean? Either she was not important enough to guard or they didn't think she could escape.

The stink grew stronger but also changed as she walked along the damp, stone floor under what was probably the last remaining portion of the old wooden roof. Now it smelled less like unflushed toilet and more like rotting apples. Of course, she realized, they probably didn't have flushable toilets in this place where people rode elephants instead of driving cars. So they would probably have to perfume things.

The scent changed again. It smelled like skunk mixed with the odor that comes to you to let you know you've stepped in dog poo. She didn't want to go toward it, but it grew stronger in the direction she wanted to go, toward the center of the castle, to a room she'd caught a glimpse of on the way to the cell. She'd seen what looked like a throne in it. That crowned fox who'd arrested her had darted into it on the way by. It was probably where she needed to go to find this Lady Mumps. It didn't take long to get used to the scent even as it changed—so that was okay. It got stronger, but at the same time less awful to her nose. The perfume of rotten apple turned to a perfume of rotting roses. And that dampened the stink a little.

The smell led her down the stone hallway to a double-wide doorway that appeared to lead into a large room with just a little bit of broken roof over a broken throne. It had only one window, but it was huge, like a movie screen. It took up half the exterior wall, but it didn't have any glass. It didn't look like it was supposed to have glass.

This was the room she remembered. It had thick wood doors that were open wide, and it was unguarded. Inside it, someone was talking. Samantha stood in the doorway, not hiding or announcing herself.

She could not see the whole space, but there appeared to be only one person in the room, a large, little woman with faded orange hair in a long, very pink gown. The gown was airy and flowing and the fabric didn't appear to be fabric that would keep out the cold. But the woman didn't show any sign of cold. She was so marvelously insulated. She was standing in front of a squat, gold-framed mirror beside the broken throne. It reflected her from head to toe. She was talking to herself. Samantha could see in the reflection of the mirror the woman's very chubby face, her bright purple cheeks, large, very red lips and round chin. She had an extraordinary amount of hair flying loosely a foot or more to the left and right of her head, but not even all that hair could hide the long sparkling earrings that hung like the blades of a ceiling fan from her spoon-like earlobes or the sparkles that covered her paper-white face like shaved ice. She raised a dull golden hoop over her head with two hands. Sam decided it was a crown of some sort. The woman lowered the hoop onto her very wide head. It seemed odd that the crown was so plain, no jewels or designs or any sticking-up parts. It was just a dull circle. And it didn't fit over her hair, which got squashed down as she adjusted it on her skull. This must be the Sorceress Lady Mumps.

Sam thought she was beautiful.

"I'm almost there. Really, we *are* there," the gelatinous woman explained to her image. "Just a few details. Not important details. I've really already won."

Her voice was amazingly high-pitched for a woman so large. And not at all weak. It was a strong voice. It sounded as though it would penetrate an orchestra, as though if she were on a phone call and a whole orchestra was playing, you could still hear every word she said. What a voice.

"They already love me," she said. "The real ones. The ones who want me. The ones who understand. And I've done so much already with my birds and my smoke and my elephants and my foxes and my cold cold air. So much so quickly. No one could ever have imagined it. More than anyone has ever done in such a short time."

She twisted to get a side view of herself.

"Or even a very long time. Everyone knows it. Everyone says so. Oz will be *marvelous* again. Soon. Very soon."

And she took what must have been a gallon jug of perfume and squeezed a little ball at the end of a tube, sending a cloud all over her face and through the room and in the direction of Samantha who was smiling in the doorway like a child who'd snuck home to surprise her favorite grandmother.

"Oz will be ours soon," the sorceress told her image, "and Oz is just the first step. And it's ours already. It really is."

Sam noticed her own reflection in the lower corner of the mirror. The sorceress noticed her too and at the same moment. Shoulders up, head high, Sam charged into the room before Mumps could turn around.

"Good morning, your high worshipfulness."

"Where's my snow?" the sorceress asked Sam's reflection in the mirror before spinning to face her. "Little sheet of paper on the ground. You call that snow? My grandmother could make better snow in her bathtub."

Sam hesitated for only a second. "Oh, it's coming," she said. "You can count on it." She bowed as she'd seen people do in movies, as though she had a large hat in her hand with a high feather sticking out of it. She bowed without bending her knee. It felt silly, but also right. "I've been sent by the king of the foxes to report that the south side of the castle will be cleared before lunchtime, as you ordered," she said. And then she stood up straight.

Sorceress Mumps stared at her with a baffled expression. "I never ordered that."

"Well, that doesn't surprise me. Between you and me, the king of the foxes doesn't always hear things right."

Mumps chuckled. "But he did find me this little land to conquer. That's why I keep him on, if I must be honest."

"Not everyone can be as on top of things as you, Lady Mumps."

Giggling, the sorceress looked back at the mirror and pulled a few strands of hair up over the rim of her crown.

"You are as beautiful as they say," said Sam. "It is such a pleasure to stand so near you again."

"We've met before?"

"Once, for just a minute. I'm sure you don't remember me—even though I am your loyalist follower. This is the second time I have had such good luck to be near you. I'm," and she paused, "I'm Sam the Trusty."

"Oh, of course I remember you. I remember everything." The sorceress pointed a tiny finger at her brain then smiled into her mirror. "Big, brain. Big big brain. Pink is my color," she mumbled.

"It is a color of great power. It goes great with the orange of your hair and the purple of your cheeks—better than any other color."

The sorceress smiled. "Yes, it does. You are very observant. What is your name?"

"I am Sam," she paused again, "Sam the Loyal."

"We're going to win. Today, I think. Or maybe tomorrow. You didn't happen to see a little bald guy with tin gloves on, did you? I think he's feeding my birds. No, no—he's, he's meeting a witch with a magic hat or something. Wonderful friend, Tin-Puh."

"He is on his way," she said. It was a little bit of a gamble to say that, but if the guy didn't show up, Sam was pretty sure she'd think up a good reason why she had bad information. Things just came to her that way most of the time.

"Although, I don't trust him," the sorceress added after a moment.

"Yes, he can be a tricky one. We should wait to see."

"He's bringing the dust of the Wicked Witch of the West," the sorceress whispered. "We're going to bring her back to life. He digs tunnels, you know. I don't know why anyone would dig tunnels. Who sees tunnels?"

"I'm sure there's a good reason."

"It's an important part of our strategy to conquer Oz. But why would anyone do it? But it will be wonderful when it's done. Actually it will be…" and she seemed to search for the right word.

"Marvelous?" said Sam.

"Yes. This land used to be marvelous," she said, "when it all belonged to the witch. We're going to make it marvelous again. But this time it'll belong to us."

Sam took a step closer. She wanted to sit down, but the only chair in the room was the broken throne and she knew she'd better not. She asked: "How do we know the witch won't just keep it once she's back?"

"Ah, well, there's the question, right there. That's the final solution to the problem. But it's not a problem. She will. You'll see."

And then the sound of a heavy step came in from the stone hallway. In clomped a short, old man with shiny gloves and metal shoes and a serious expression his face, and beside him came a little woman in a dirty red dress carrying a hat as though it were a bag and looking skeptical.

"So you are having the Tin Body?" said the little man without greeting. And then he noticed Sam, "And what is this child? This is not a meeting for all ears. Where is this Dox?"

"Oh, this is an old friend. She's fine. Her name is, um, ah, Sssssslappy Loyal," isn't that right, Slappy?"

"You called it," Sam smiled.

"No, I am not thinking so," the little man said.

"Slappy stays," the sorceress declared.

"I know how to get the loyalty of the Wicked Witch of the West," Sam said.

"You know about the witch?" The little woman pulled the hat close to her chest as though someone was trying to take it away.

"I know everything."

"How is this?" said the little man.

"If I tell you, I can stay?"

"Remember, I still have the tin body," said Mumps.

"Of course," the little man nodded with an unfriendly face. "I am being Tin-Puh. And this is being Witch Lloco-Monnem."

"I knew that," Sam said.

"It is certain that you did," Tin-Puh smiled grimly.

"She seems to know everything," said the sorceress. "Almost as much as me. Well done, Stinky."

"I thought she was Slappy," the red witch said.

"I'm whatever the supreme sorceress wants me to be," said Sam. "Some people call me Sam."

"Well, don't worry. No one here is going to do that," said Lady Mumps. And then she turned to Lloco-Monnem. "Is that the West Witch?"

"She's a powerful witch," said the Witch Lloco-Monnem. "We will need to control her."

"Stinky has that down," said the Lady Mumps.

"And I must to get the body of this Tin Woodman," said Tin-Puh.

"Why do you need that body, anyway?" Mumps asked. "If it's worth so much, perhaps I should just keep it."

"You are wanting my services," said Tin-Puh.

"Well why do you want it?"

Tin-Puh looked at Sam as though he expected her to say something. But Sam said nothing. "As you can see, I have been attempting to convert myself to tin. I have elbows and the feet. But not real elbows." And he pulled an elbow covering off to show he had his own flesh-and-blood elbow underneath. "And they are not yet tin either." He pulled the magnet off his hat and put it back on.

"This I have is but armor. In my country, it will be very useful to be having this undying tin body."

"But you don't want the head?" said Mumps.

"Why would I be wanting the head when I am having *this* head? One does not conquer this world with tin head."

"Let's everyone take a seat," the sorceress said, and she sat on the red cushion of the broken throne. Everyone else stood.

Just then, Dox the Fox King panted in.

"My sovereign, my apologies. But our prisoners have escaped. I would have been here already but I have been flogging the derelict guards and... and," and then he looked at Sam. "How did you get out?"

Sam looked at Lady Mumps and made a sign for "crazy," and then she said to the fox king, "I've delivered your message about our extraordinary progress on the south side."

Dox scratched his head, and then he looked at all the faces. "Well, actually, I mean, there are some stumps and stones that are..." If he was hoping some face would reveal the best direction for this speech, he was disappointed. "But that doesn't matter," he said. "Guards, guards, I've located an escapee. Come arrest her." Two guards rushed into the room.

"Stand back," the sorceress yelled. "No one arrests Sloppy Loyal—Sloppy?—Stoppy? No one arrests my loyal friend unless I say so. Don't make me get out of this chair."

"But Lady."

The guards stopped in their tracks several steps from Sam.

"Did I ever tell you why we're taking over Oz?" the sorceress asked the whole room, picking up a slice of cake from the side table where she kept her cosmetics.

"Often," said the fox king.

"It's because great people need to be admired, and if they're great they need to be admired greatly. And the greatest of all need to be admired the greatest-est of all. We need to be where people worship us, because we need to be worshipped, because we are great. People are mostly pretty stupid. They don't know greatness when they see it. The smart ones do. We don't have to worry about them. Now, Slappy Loyal here is one of the smart ones. She knows. We don't put people like that in jail. You understand?" The sorceress fluffed up her hair and puffed out her sleeves. "The rest of the people, we have to control them."

"You think people are idiots but you want them to worship you?" Loco-Monnem asked. "And what if they don't?"

"Then we kill them."

"Well, that might to cause resentment in the people," Tin-Puh observed. "Unless you are doing it so carefully."

"People make these things out to be more complicated than they are," Lady Mumps took another bite of cake.

"How do you know this will work," Lloco-Monnem wondered.

"Because I figured it out. See this head? I have a big brain inside it. And I figured it out in my big brain."

"Ah, but, you see…"

"Why don't you like brains? Brains are where people think. And the biggest brains think the biggest thoughts. And I have the biggest brain, and that means—chocolate."

"What?" said the witch.

"I just… You there,. Fox guard, I need a piece of chocolate cake. Go get me one."

One of the foxes ran from the room.

"But you have one in your hand," said the fox king.

The sorceress ran to the door. "Make it the biggest piece you've ever seen," she yelled down the hallway, throwing the plate with the cake out of the room. "I have no such thing," she said, turning back into the room.

The sorceress returned to her throne. Everyone in the room was silent, as though no one knew what to say. It was as though a foul-smelling fog was growing in the space among them.

Sam understood. She needed to clear the air. So she said the first thing that came into her head: "You know what I've always wondered, if I may ask, is why Oz? Your wisdom is greater than all wisdom by leaps and bounds. But your choice of the world's weirdest country—I don't get it."

A harried fox ran in at moment with another slice of cake.

"The dessert," the lady said.

Everyone looked baffled.

"It's a deadly barrier," said Mumps.

"Oh," said Dox. "You mean the desert. The deadly desert, the one that surrounds Oz," said Dox.

"Anyone who tries to cross it gets turned to sugar," Mumps said. "What a great idea."

"Sand," said Dox. "They turn to sand."

"I thought of it myself," Mumps said. "You see, it's already got a border around it, like frosting." She lifted the slice of cake with her little hand and took a bite. "I don't have to build it. And it's a perfect barrier. No one can get past it."

"But all we have got past it," Tin-Puh said, pointing one after another to everyone in the room.

"Impenetrable," the Sorceress Lady Mumps said. "Where's my cake?"

Sixteen

"We're better off without it," Thaddeus said. But Louise did not agree.

"It's the Love Magnet," she said.

"Didn't you notice, no one loved us the whole time we had it. It's like reverse magic."

"It says *A Love Magnet* right on it."

"The whole time we had it, no one even liked us."

"He's right about that," Mildred said. "It wasn't doing us any good."

"I just don't believe that," said Thaddeus.

Mildred wanted to tell Thaddeus *he'd* seen magic and didn't believe in it, but that didn't seem like the best thing to say at the moment. So, instead, she said, "but we *do* have to get it back to get home."

"But I've already said that's not true," said Louise. "Ozma…"

"Obviously those silly books don't help us much in the real Oz," Thaddeus said.

"Silly?" Louise stared hard at Thaddeus from the tops of her eyes.

"They do have rubber mountains in them, spinning rubber mountains that people bounce off," said Mildred.

Louise crossed her arms.

"People often lose their temper when they are scared," Mildred said. "It's best to focus on what we have to do now and not to fight. Things will look different if we wait." Mildred didn't look at either Thaddeus or Louise as she said this. She seemed to be talking to the ground.

"Okay," said Louise. "The question is, what do we do now?"

"We need to find a way home." Thaddeus just folded his arms.

"To do that, we need to find Ozma," said Louise.

Mildred was glad to see she'd calmed everyone down.

"But first we need to get the magnet back."

"Agreed," said Louise.

"Why would we need to do that?" said Thaddeus.

"Because it brought us here," said Mildred.

"Because Oz is more dangerous than I thought," said Louise.

"And so if the books aren't completely accurate," said Mildred, "then we don't know if Ozma can get us home. But we do know that the magnet can."

But Thaddeus said, "That's just not possible. There's nothing in science…"

And then Louise said, "Maybe science doesn't help that much in the real Oz."

And Mildred said, "Okay, just…" But Louise and Thaddeus didn't listen to her.

"Science says you have to accept the simplest explanation that covers all the facts," said Thaddeus. "Fact one: everyone who sees us hates us."

"The Love Magnet can't make people *hate* you," said Louise.

"But it doesn't make people love us," said Thaddeus.

"You don't know what people would have been like if we didn't have it."

"Perfect time to find out," said Thaddeus. "I say we need to give up on the magnet and look for this Ozma character."

"But no," said Mildred, "I just said…"

"I agree with Mildred," said Louise.

"But if it doesn't make people love us and we don't need it to get home, why do we even want to get it back?" said Thaddeus.

"It's two against one," Mildred said.

"But for dumb reasons," Thaddeus said. "You want it back because you think it makes people like us, but it doesn't. And she wants it back because she thinks we need it to get home, but we don't."

"It's not about reasons, it's about voting," said Mildred.

Trees rustled with a sound stronger than wind. They all looked to the left and saw a line of moving color behind a wall of green leaves.

"What's that?" Louise whispered.

"Who's there?" came a voice from the other side of the green.

"Shhhhhhh," said Mildred.

"COME on TELL us your NAMES," said a strange and mechanical voice.

Louise's jaw dropped. "Tik-Tok," she said aloud.

"Is it a bomb?" Thaddeus said. And then the loud roar of a lion flooded the air.

Mildred froze. So did Thaddeus. Louise laughed. Thaddeus looked at Louise like she was crazy.

"It's the Cowardly Lion," Louise said.

A hole formed in the line of trees and an eyeless patchwork head pushed through. "I don't see anything," it said.

"Your eyes are in your pocket," said a voice the children had not heard before.

The patchwork head pulled back and the green space closed.

"We should go see them, c'mon," Louise said. And as she took a step forward, the space in the wall of leaves opened again, and the head of the Tin Woodman in the Patchwork Girl's quilted hands poked through.

"It's them," it said.

"Run," said the lion. The head disappeared from the wall of leaves and the sound of feet moving with all possible speed followed immediately. Before the children could decide to pursue, they were gone.

"See, look what happens when we don't have the magnet," Louise said.

"The same thing that happened when we did have the magnet," Thaddeus said. "People just don't like us."

"But that was the Patchwork Girl, and the Cowardly Lion, and the Tin Woodman. They like everyone," said Louise.

"And we're the good guys," Mildred said.

"Everyone thinks they're the good guys," Thaddeus said.

"That was the worst encounter yet," Mildred said.

"Because we don't have the magnet," Louise said.

Seventeen

"I think we lost 'em," said Scraps.

"I must say, they didn't look nasty," said the Tin Head.

"Oh, they never do," said Scraps.

"I think someone needs to sew your eyes back on," the Wogglebug said, rubbing his arms as he climbed off the back of the lion.

"Maybe you should try putting yours in your pocket," said the Patchwork Girl, holding an eye toward the magnified insect.

"My legs are moving," the Tin Head said.

"You don't have any legs." Professor Wogglebug passed his hand under the Tin Head like a magician.

"Those must be *my* legs," said Scraps, who was carrying the head under her arm.

"No, no," said the Tin Head. "I do have legs. They're just not attached. And yours are not moving, and I can feel my legs moving, somewhere. And my arms as well. I wonder where I am."

"Who's moving them?" asked the Lion.

"I don't know. Let me try something." And a look of concentration passed over his tin face as everybody watched.

"Can you do it?" Scraps asked.

"Not easily. It feels like someone is trying to push my body in one direction while I try to move it in another."

"Well I'm sure it's that Witch Mumpty Mumps."

"The SOR-cer-ESS la-DY mumps," said Tik-Tok.

"Whatever," said Scraps. "Don't let her push you around. Whatever direction she pushes you, push in a different one. You might run into walls, but you won't be turned into furniture."

"PLUS, she is FLESH and BLOOD and will TIRE if you RE-sist."

"Good idea," said the Tin Head.

Eighteen

The Scarecrow Man zig-zagged down the hall like an acorn bouncing off branches as it ricochets to the far-off ground. It took all his willpower and all his pointy brains to maintain his forward direction and also not to dent the Tin Woodman's body on the rough stones. He put his right foot forward only to have his left foot pull him back, and so he tumbled onto his stomach or butt. Once or twice, he tried to crawl, but he only rolled around like a badly weighted can of beans. Then, suddenly, for a moment, when he had managed to pull himself up onto the Tin Woodman's feet again, everything was okay. He took several easy steps forward. Oh, but then the fit hit him again, and he found himself hopping and rattling when he wanted to be lightly stepping so no one would hear he was there. No matter how hard he tried, he couldn't keep the body under control for more than a few steps.

The body had not been so willful when he first found the Tin Woodman's ax under that pile of straw. He'd felt little tugs and pulls, but he mostly had it under control. Just after putting it on, the body did what he wanted it to do. He swung the ax quite easily. And he almost laughed to feel such strength in his arms—something his straw arms had never felt before. And although it felt odd to have arms so stiff, and he knew he'd miss the flexibility of his own straw-filled sleeves if he had to wear such strong arms too long, still, how wonderful it was to be so strong, to swing a heavy ax with ease and see the wood chips fly. He had the door open in no time. He looked around carefully, saw that his banging had drawn no one's attention, and strolled into the wide, stone hallway.

But then the body stopped working. One moment he was enjoying the sensation of a body that marched with military ease, and the next he was spastic, hopping, running, crawling, hurtling forwards, backwards and in circles, bumping and scraping—making very slow, very noisy progress. If anyone heard him, he probably would not manage to find a way out of the castle. And he desperately wanted to find his way back to his friends.

At that same time, in the forest outside the castle, the Tin Woodman's head was still thinking about the odd sensation he'd been having all morning, the sensation of swinging arms and moving legs. What was going on? Was his body really moving somewhere without him? If so, he should take the advice of his friends and try to get control of it, get it out of the castle and safe from the thieving hands of that crazy Mumps lady or, even worse, that body-thief Tin-Puh. He imagined his body in the space of the castle's stone hallways. He tried hard to remember the last corridor he was in before his head was removed, and then he imagined himself moving through it. He wished he'd paid more attention to where the turns were—but there really were a lot of turns in that mountain and that castle. Still, he was determined. Perhaps, with luck or diligence, he could get his body to come and meet him here in the woods.

"The hallways of that castle must be very short and jagged," the Tin Head said to his companions. "I can't go two steps in any direction without hitting something."

"I have the same problem," said Scraps.

"Maybe if you took your eyes out of your pocket," said the Wogglebug.

"I'm trying to get my body to move like a kite so I can look down on everyone and laugh," Scraps said.

"Why would you want to do that?" asked the Lion.

"Flying and laughing? Two of my favorite things. Hey, Tik-Tok, see how far you could toss me into the air."

"NO time now. MAYbe laTER."

"I am sure the distance between the head and the heart would be your problem," the Wogglebug said to the Tin Head. "The body should be proximate to the head for easy regulation of the limbs." The Wogglebug was talking kind of slowly.

"Or you could just pull on 'em," said Scraps, who offered to pull on one of the professor's appendages.

The Tin Head paused to think about that.

"The professor is probably right," said the Head. "It's hard to move without having eyes attached to the body."

"Speak for yourself," said Scraps who had been climbing up the clockwork man and at that moment launched herself heedlessly from the top of his head. She did not get very high before she floated with arms and legs outspread back to the ground.

In the castle, the Scarecrow Man felt control come back to the tin body. He took a few steps forward and would have smiled afresh to feel this body obeying his desires if his painted mouth were not already settled into a perfectly acceptable grin. Hearing voices in a room up ahead, he stopped so they would not hear him. The door led into to the broken throne room where the Sorceress Lady Mumps had ordered him and the Tin Woodman disassembled. He could hear the scratchy sound of her piercing pipes. But who was with her?

"Tell me the plan again," Mumps squeaked.

"Imagine this," said a voice. The Scarecrow Man peered in the room cautiously. Dox, Tin-Puh, and Samantha were standing in a semi-circle in front of the seated pink sorceress. And there was another person there, one he'd never seen before, a Quadling-sized woman in a soiled red dress. Dox was talking.

"Imagine the Great Princess, Ozma herself, ancient girl sovereign of all Oz, sitting on her Emerald Throne. She's telling Jellia Jamb, her maid, and Thurbidore, her palace guard, about the strange disturbance in the Winkie lands. Winkie ambassador Sakem enters the room to assure everyone the esteemed Emperor Nick Chopper, the Tin Woodman, has everything under control. Ozma breathes a sigh of relief. But just then, out of nowhere, she feels a little bit of a rumbling. Then a little bit more. It is something she has never felt before. She runs to the window. She stares out from her high perch on all the Emerald City. Down below the frightened citizens are running in circles, bumping into each other."

"When did that happen?" the sorceress squeaked.

"It has not to happen yet," said Tin-Puh.

"That's why you were asked to *imagine* it," said the Quadling woman.

"I see," said the sorceress.

"In the Emerald City," Dox continued, "they are yelling, 'what is it? What do we do?' The streets rumble, and now they start to shake. Large buildings pitch. Bricks come loose all over the city and fall from great heights onto the unprotected hats of the panicky citizens. Ozma sees Frogman, just visiting from the country of the Yips, barely dodge one brick only to be slapped between the eyes by another. She sees the beloved Woozie trampled by frightened people. The ground is strewn with smashed green glasses, and then bricks and emeralds fall like rain, like a storm: The Wooden Sawhorse is splintered. The Hungry Tiger is smashed. Billina the chicken and all her chicks are flattened."

"Oooo, that must've hurt," said the sorceress.

"It will when is happening," said Tin-Puh.

"We haven't done this yet?" the sorceress said.

"Listen," said Dox. "Imagine it. That is just the beginning. Panic grows. The shaking continues while underneath the great city, the last supports are pulled free and the whole metropolis sinks into the ground with such a cacophonous rant that in moments not one brick sits upon another. Ozma cascades down to the floor of the city and then down and down into the pit of the worn-out ground until she lacks the strength to climb the rubble back to the surface."

"So she's probably dead," said the sorceress. "So why haven't we declared victory."

"None of this has happened, yet," said the Quadling.

"*Imagine* it," said Dox.

"Yeah, I don't know what that means. Tell me more," said the sorceress.

"It's quite a mess, don't you think?" said Dox. "But it doesn't end there. At the first rumbling, every fox and elephant in Oz begins the march to the capital. We give the defeated Ozites time to ache and stew and dig the first crumpled bodies from the ruins. And then we arrive: Lady Mumps on a high chair atop the biggest elephant in Oz. And the incomparable Tin-Puh at the Elephant to his right, and the Witch Lloco-Monnem on the elephant to his left and me, King Dox, on my own elephant, riding in front."

"You do like to listen to your own self when you are speaking," Tin-Puh said without a smile.

"Why are you in the front?" said Mumps.

"In the front but lower down, on little tiny elephant, to make you seem all the more impressive," said Dox.

"I go first," Mumps declared.

"As you wish," said Dox.

"Tell me more."

"Staring down into the deep well of the ruined city, we tell Ozma no one can help her."

"I thought she was dead," said Mumps.

"Oz," said Dox, "nobody dies. We tell her we have undermined not just her capital, but every city and every important town in Oz. We've sunk the pumpkin house of her son. We've flattened the castle of the Winkie emperor and the chateau of the Red Sorceress. We mention the shattering of the tinkling China Country. We tell her of how much more we will do if she does not relinquish her throne."

"Oh, goody," said Mumps. "Then what did she say?"

"And then, then—when the sovereign of Oz is in deepest confusion," the Quadling woman said, "we unleash the revived Wicked Witch, who soars over the devastated city on her broom." She placed the upside-down, black witch's hat on a table near the throne. And she dug her hand into it and grabbed a handful of tawny dust."

"I like it," said Mumps. "But are we sure we need to bring back this witch? Slappy here is worried about that."

"I'm afraid we do," said Dox. "Once Ozma is defeated, we need her to take over on the throne of the Emerald City."

"Hey," Mumps' jaw dropped. "*I'm* supposed to take over. And I get to carry that cool stick with the O-Z on the top. And wear that gold tiara. It'll be great. Big crowds will shout my name. Big, big crowds." And a monstrous grin crawled across her face. And then she grabbed the bag of witch dust and was about to turn it over. "So, no witches!"

"No, no, no," said Tin-Puh, taking the bag from Mumps' hands. "We have already to have explained it. The people are knowing this witch already. They shall to accept her. We need this witch as puppet at beginning, for to keep scared."

"Then," Dox added, "once we have the people cowed and afraid, we just dump a bucket of water over her head, and you take over."

"Then I get the tiara?"

"Yes."

"And the stick?"

"And also the stick," Tin-Puh said.

"Okay, then." Mumps reached her face down ner the hatful of dust and snorted and sneezed. "So how we we bring her back?"

"Well, that is the question," said Lloco-Monnem. "It appears to be a three-step process: the first step is to collect the dust, which I've done. The second is to bring the dust to where it was dissolved— and here it is in this castle. The next part is the problem. We need to find a magic talisman."

"A what?" asked Mumps.

"According to Glinda's book, which I read before I magiced it, somewhere in this castle is a device that stirs the dust back to life."

"Where? What does it look like?" Mumps clasped her hands together.

"It didn't say. But I do think we'll know it when we see it. It will react to the dust immediately. It should not be hard to find."

"So we just carry the hat around the castle until it starts doing stuff?"

Just then in the woods, the Tin Head, having felt no movement in his limbs for some time, thought he'd try to move his body again. And in the castle, the body with the scarecrow head lurched noisily into the doorway. It stopped for just a moment. And then at a dead run it threw the Scarecrow Man sprawling onto the floor where he sailed forward with such force that he slid into the center of the room like a flat stone on wet ice. He rattled to a stop at the feet of Tin-Puh and the Witch Lloco-Monnem. The Sorceress Mumps shrieked like a baby pig and barely managed to pull her great bulk out of the way as the Scarecrow Man skidded near.

As soon as the body came to a stop, the Scarecrow Man twisted his head around. Five faces stared down at him.

"My body," said Tin-Puh.

"Not even *my* body," said the Scarecrow Man. "I'm sure it's not yours."

"Not yet," said Mumps. "Who let this loser out? Get this thing back under guard and then cut off the head of whoever let it escape."

"I let myself escape," said the Scarecrow Man, his feet flailing as he lay on the floor, his head turned all the way around. "And the head can be removed without cutting, although I would prefer for now to leave it attached."

Dox and the Witch Lloco-Monnem bent down to lift the body, trying to avoid the legs and feet that were moving like the legs of a rolled-over turtle.

"You could help," said Dox to the Scarecrow Man.

"I don't know that I could. I clearly haven't begun to master the knees."

The Tin Man in the forest said, "It's like trying to get through a maze in the dark. I feel I've fallen down. And now I feel I'm getting up. And now I feel like I'm not getting up."

"I'll put my eyes back in my pocket and tell you where to go," said Scraps.

"Well, it shall be mine soon," said Tin-Puh in the castle. "Not to scratch it."

"If you earn it," said Mumps. "More updates. How's the undermining going?"

"The first step is nearly complete."

"First step?"

"Well, we have finished to undermine the capital, this City of Emeralds. We can make it to fall at a moment. And, for more assurance, your enemies are intercepted," Tin-Puh said.

"What enemies?"

"The scrap quilt, the bug monster, and the copper robot, and also the unworthy lion. And I did disarm the children as well."

"Children? What children? I hate children."

"These three I have met in the woods. They have been armed with this." Tin-Puh pulled the magnet off his funnel hat.

"A horseshoe magnet?" said Mumps.

"They want it, so I keep it," said Tin-Puh.

"Oh, I've seen these children," said the Witch Lloco-Monnem. "We do not want this toy. It is a...."

"It's a Love Magnet," said Sam, who had been waiting to speak. "It brought us to Oz."

"So, then you are of these troublesome children?" Tin-Puh narrowed his eyes.

"No, no, they kidnapped me. But I overpowered them and escaped."

"Another unlikeable child," said the Witch Lloco-Monnem. "A love magnet would be useless to us."

"I do not agree with this," said Tin-Puh. "Is there more powerful weapon than this love?"

"Why would we want to love people?" the sorceress asked.

"No, no," Tin-Puh said. "You are not protected from love when you are having it. But people, they love you. Think what you can make them to do? Think of the time it shall save after this undermining is completed."

"But where's the fun in that?" Dox wanted to know.

Lloco-Monnem reached for the magnet with a look of confusion on her face that Tin-Puh asked her about.

"If this is the children's magnet, I don't think it works. They told me they had it. But I did not like them, not at all." She took the magnet from Tin-Puh's hand. She turned it over and read the inscription: "A" on one tine "Love" on the bottom and "Magnet" on the other tine. Then she rubbed her calloused thumb along one of the tines scraping away little bits of paint, dirt and rust. Then, to improve the light, she walked to the wide empty window overlooking the courtyard. She licked the dirtiest part of the magnet and put it in her mouth like a lollypop. Pulling it out, she held it back up to the light. Then she beckoned the others over to the light and showed them the magnet.

"This is no *Love* Magnet." She passed it in front of their eyes. "It is an *Anti*-Love Magnet."

"No," said Tin-Puh.

"That, I like," said the sorceress.

"Like sand on a desert," said Dox.

"You don't need one of those to not like Mildred," said Sam.

Tin-Puh took the magnet back from the witch and walked back to the throne and tossed it on the table by the hat. "Then it is being useless," he said.

A roar like the rush of wind down a narrow alley filled the room. Out the window, billows of black smoke rose. Tin-Puh went back to the window to watch.

"It comes from a furnace in the mountain," Mumps shouted with theatrical movements of her arms, "then it goes through a gigantical chimney behind that wall over there, across from the throne, and out through the middle of the castle. Pretty brilliant. We let it fill the sky until it's time to call back the birds. Just lovely."

"This we know," Tin-Puh said.

"Just add birds," said Mumps.

None of them was thinking of the Scarecrow Man. He sat up. The Tin Woodman's body was once again under his control. He quietly scanned the room. Mumps, Tin-Puh, Lloco-Monnem and Dox all stood with their backs to him, staring out at the spreading smoke and holding their ears against the roar. The Scarecrow Man rose to his feet unnoticed. This would be a good time to leave. He glanced at the Anti-Love Magnet on the table beside the hat full of powder. Around it, a cloud of dust was forming. The dust had risen out of the hat, speck by speck, and was beginning to spin like a little cyclone around the tines of the magnet. He grabbed the magnet, turned to see that he was still not being watched and made his way as quietly as he could back into the hallway.

In the woods, the Tin Head gave up trying to move his body in the dark. "Whoever is moving my body does not easily tire," he said.

Nineteen

Black smoke billowed out from the castle and spread in all directions. Huge flocks of twittering birds swarmed against it. They dimmed the sun. The air grew colder. Wogglebugs in the wild do not survive temperatures like these. But fortunately for the professor, this was Oz. And he just slowly froze— or rather almost froze. His limbs slowed down. He found himself unable to walk and barely able to talk. But this did not much matter because his brain function slowed too, leaving him little to say. It started to snow.

"Quick," called the Patchwork Girl, her button eyes at the ends of her fingers, "find his key; wind him up."

Nearby and unseen, the children were rubbing their arms and hitting their legs and making themselves as small as they could. Thick clouds of mist poured from their mouths.

"I'm cold," said Thaddeus.

"We're all cold," said Mildred.

"We have to run," said Louise.

"I don't want to run," said Mildred.

Louise put a hand on Mildred's back and another on Thaddeus' shoulder and pushed. "There are no houses nearby," she said. "And no one will take us in anyway. We have to run to get warm." And so they ran.

Tik-Tok swiveled his head at the sound of movement in the bushes. Scraps put her buttons in her pocket and raised the Tin Man's head and said, "tell me what you see." The Cowardly Lion shivered, got behind the Clockwork Man, crouched and peered around his legs. The Wogglebug just stood there.

"Something's coming," said the Tin Head.

"And us without weapons," said the Lion.

"WE have a LI-ON," said Tik-Tok.

"And a pointy Tin Head," said Scraps.

But it was only children, running.

"Roar," Tik-Tok said. And the Lion roared. "ROAR a-GAIN," said the Clockwork Man. And the Lion roared even louder. And the running children ran away without approaching.

"Did I scare them?" asked the Lion.

"Okay," said Thaddeus, still running, "this is nothing like any Oz I've ever heard of."

"He's not supposed to be scary," Louise said.

"This is *so* different," said Mildred.

They were all feeling a little warmer now, but they kept running. They had almost run out of energy when they heard the great roar of the lion, but when they heard that noise they found they had a whole new tank of energy in reserve, and they kept running until the lion and the others were out of sound or sight.

Mildred was the first one to slow down, followed almost immediately by Thaddeus. Louise could have kept going, but when Mildred panted, "stop," she was just as glad to stop.

"I think we're safe."

"We're not safe," Thaddeus panted. "It's snowing again. And we don't have any food. And now I'm all sweaty and that's going to freeze. And we don't know where we are."

"She means from the lion," said Mildred.

"Have you seen the lion?" said a voice. And they all turned their heads. They'd come to the edge of the woods. Just in front of them was a wide open plain, and beyond that a dark castle. The plain was just then filling up with elephants and foxes, a few of which seemed to be lumbering in their direction. But just in front of them was the strangest creature they'd yet seen in Oz: a barrel-bodied, cloth-headed creature. It looked to the children like someone had thrown together a Halloween costume at the last minute out of old costumes they'd found lying around.

"I'm looking for the Lion," the creature stopped right in front of the group.

"He's not very nice," said Thaddeus.

"Why do you say that?" asked the creature.

"Are you the Tin Man or the Scarecrow?" Louise asked.

"At the moment I'm a little of both," said the Scarecrow Man. "I need to find the Tin Woodman's head so I can return his body and then put my own back together. But why do you say the Lion is unkind?"

"He roared at us like he wanted to eat us?"

"Perhaps he was scared," said the Scarecrow Man. "Sometimes people roar when they are scared."

"Of us?"

"It's true that I see nothing scary in a group of children, but the Cowardly Lion is scared more easily than I am. He's more destructible, you know."

"How come you like us?" said Mildred.

"Why would I not like children?"

Behind the Scarecrow Man, the elephants were getting closer. The ground began to rumble beneath the stomping of their feet. A din rose from the foxes driving them with deep voices and loud whips.

"Please take me to the Lion," said the Scarecrow Man, "I assure you he will not hurt you, and we can talk as we go."

"Since we arrived in Oz, no one has liked us," said Thaddeus.

"That is because you were carrying an Anti-Love Magnet."

"Huh?"

The Scarecrow Man told them what he'd heard in the castle.

"Really?"

"Wow."

Just then a voice, like a voice of joy called down from overhead. Everyone looked up to see the Patchwork Girl, like a swift cloud made from the stuff of a rainbow, sail over their heads, her arms and legs spread wide. She landed just a few feet away with no more whoosh than a leaf makes.

"Do it again," she said.

"Who are you talking to?" said the Scarecrow Man.

"Wait, where are my eyes. Oh, of..." and then she stopped and pulled an eye out of her pocket. "Scarecrow?"

"Sort of," he said.

"I was talking to the Lion. He balled me up and threw me. It was great fun."

"Perhaps not wise, though," said the Scarecrow Man.

"But now I don't feel so happy," she said. "I feel cold. And I can't feel cold. Isn't that funny."

The trees rustled and the Cowardly Lion leaped in front of them. He crouched for a moment as though he were planning to leap on prey. The children cringed. Then the lion sniffed the air and stood up tall.

"You're not scary," he said. And then he noticed the Scarecrow Man.

A moment later Tik-Tok's heavy step came through the bushes. The lion looked the Scarecrow Man up and down.

"Aren't you glad to see me, old friend?"

"Not as glad as you'd think," he said. "Perhaps it is the stiffness of your clothing."

"Oh, my," said Scraps, who by then had both of her eye buttons in her hands, "It must be awful."

"It's not so bad," said the Scarecrow Man, who seemed to understand exactly what she meant. "I would not want this body always, but it works for the Tin Woodman. And it's wonderfully strong. But it does take some getting used to. I still don't quite know how he gets it to cooperate."

Just then the Wogglebug came stiffly through the underbrush carrying the Tin Man's head.

"My friend," said the Tin Head.

"And your body too," said the Scarecrow Man.

"This is so cool," Louise said.

Mildred and Thaddeus just looked at each other.

As the Scarecrow was reassembled with the straw and clothes that were hidden inside the Tin Woodman's hollow chest and the Tin Woodman's head was quickly re-secured on the barrel body, the children told the group what the Scarecrow had told them just moments before, a story the Scarecrow corrected and added to once he had his old body back until everyone knew everything that he'd overheard in the castle. And once he was finished, the children told their story of how the magnet found them and how they got to Oz and everything that had happened since. And while they were all telling their stories the Scarecrow and the Patchwork Girl hugged the children and the Lion licked their faces and the Tin Woodman rubbed their heads and everyone said how sorry they were that they had had to go through all that misery because of the Anti-Love Magnet.

"Well," said the Wogglebug. "I must say, now that we are all safe together, our quest is done. Thanks to the intrepid Scarecrow we have all the information we need to report to the princess, and let her take it from here."

"But WHERE IS the MAG-net NOW?" Tik-Tok asked.

"Yeah," said Scraps. "Nobody hates you."

The Scarecrow said to the Tin Woodman, "I thought I put it in your hand."

The Tin Woodman found his hands empty.

"But you notice that the children liked you right away," said the Lion.

"Must be those unflexy tin hands," said the Patchwork Girl. "He dropped it."

"It *is* hard to hold sometimes," said Mildred.

"We must have lost it, all right," said the Scarecrow and Tin Woodman.

In all the joy of meeting and talking, no one noticed that the snow had stopped, and the day was growing warmer. The smoke from the castle had cleared and the screaming birds returned from the ends of the Winkie country and the unblocked sun had risen higher and the day felt more like a brisk fall than a deep winter, and the Wogglebug had got his easy movement, most of his voice, and much of his thinking back. "Oh," he said. "That may be a complication. If I understand your story properly, the magnet *wanted* to go to the castle, and it found a way to do it."

"Yeah," said Scraps. "I'll bet it skedaddled like a witch from water back into the evil castle."

"Or SOMEwhere beTWEEN HERE AND there."

So there was not enough time to return to the Emerald City to tell Ozma what they'd learned. They all agreed they had to get the magnet out the castle before it found its way to the dust of the Wicked Witch.

"And also rescue Sam," said Mildred.

Twenty

ox the Fox King and the Sorceress Mumps were quarreling over strategy.

"If you want something to be true, just say that it's true until they believe you," said the lady in pink, waving her hand as though she were holding a magic wand.

"I know that," said Dox, "but it helps if you have something that looks like evidence."

Mumps laughed. The Witch Lloco-Monnem also laughed, although not convincingly.

"We can always be making that," said Tin-Puh, "just words."

They were all looking out through the throne room window into the bright Land of Oz beyond the edge of the black smoke: faraway blue hills, purple fields of flowers. Sam turned her back to the window and looked back to where the Scarecrow Man should have been.

"He's gone," she said.

No one heard her. Mumps told Dox they'd never get everyone in the world to do whatever they tell them to do if they used up all their time rooting around for evidence. The Witch Lloco-Monnem chucklingly said how wise Tin-Puh had been to choose an invisible country surrounded by a deadly desert. "Once we have this place under control, we can go anywhere we want. No one will be able to find us." Mumps mentioned that it was actually her idea. They all squabbled about whose idea it was until Sam repeated, "He's gone. He ran away." And she ran over to where the Scarecrow Man had been. "And I think he took the magnet."

Tin-Puh heard that. "You let him go away," he yelled. By "you" he meant Mumps. But Mumps decided he meant Sam.

"Traitor," Mumps yelled at Sam.

"No, no," said Sam.

"You gave him my magnet. You told him to run," Mumps screeched.

"He heard all our plans," said Lloco-Monnem.

"You sold us to the enemy," Mumps ranted.

"Arrest her," yelled Dox.

"Hey," Sam yelled back, "I'm the one that just told you he escaped."

"Death," said Dox, "as a lesson for everyone."

Tin-Puh said nothing.

"Actually, what she said almost makes sense," said Lloco-Monnem.

"What difference does that make?" Dox asked. "Executions can be very useful." He pulled a knife from his belt.

"How about if I just find the magnet and bring back the weirdo before he tells anyone?" Sam said.

"I don't think so," said Mumps.

But Sam turned and ran out of the room. No one tried to stop her. Dox slashed the air with a lazy wave of his knife.

"We can always execute her later if we want to," Mumps said.

Sam was soon hopelessly lost in the maze of corridors in the old castle. Baffled at how quickly Mumps had turned on her, she asked every fox she passed how to get out of the castle. They all pointed down. She descended. If she could find the magnet and bring back the thief, they would have to see that she was on their side. And how hard could that be? The Scarecrow Man was not powerful or clever. And he certainly wouldn't move very fast in that rigid tin suit. But getting out of the castle proved difficult, and it took a long time. She descended stairways and ran through hallways and passed slowly through dim empty tunnels, never sure she was any closer to the exit. Now and then there was another fox who gave her directions. But these seemed only to confuse matters. There seemed to be nothing much in the mountain besides these corridors or tunnels—just a few rooms with locked doors and one large furnace where they burned the trees that the foxes and elephants were cutting to make thick smoke and another big room where injured foxes and elephants went to heal. She'd wandered a long way before she found even those places. The foxes' directions sent her back and forth so many times that even the slow tin can, if he knew where to go, certainly would have had time enough to get some distance away before she stumbled upon the exit.

Outside at last, Sam breathed cold air at the base of the mountain. She shivered. But she knew she must not waste time wishing she had a coat. She had to find the weirdo. But where? That scarecrow-headed tin can could be anywhere. She looked at the ground in hopes of seeing tracks in the dirt.

There were no tracks. But there was a magnet. So he *had* made it out. He must have dropped the magnet. Yes, it was the Anti-Love Magnet. She could go back with that, and maybe that would make the pink sorceress praise her again. But, thinking of how angry she had been—as angry as her own mother had been when she'd shown her her last report card on the same day she got that call from the principal about "playground behavior"—she doubted that the magnet would be enough to make Mumps like her again. She said she'd bring the weirdo back, and she would have to do that. He was still dangerous.

The first elephants she found outside had not seen him.

"But he must have come by here."

The elephants and foxes moved around a lot. And they weren't interested in anything that wasn't right at the end of their snouts or trunks. So, with the next fox she tried a different question: what direction had Tin-Puh come from? Tin-Puh had seen Mildred and her friends on his way. So whatever way that was, that was probably the way she needed to go. That question was easily answered. A trim fox in a fur coat atop a burly elephant pointed just to the left of the sun. She put the magnet deep in her pocket and headed toward the edge of the freshly cleared forest.

Soon, just as she was about to take a step into the line of trees, she heard voices—and one was saying her name.

"Well, that was easy," she said aloud but soft.

The voice who said her name was Mildred's. Had Mildred said any other thing than what she actually said, Sam would have paused to listen for more, hoping to figure out who was with Mildred and what they were up to. But hearing her own name spoken, she couldn't stop herself from yelling in the direction of the speaker, "What do you mean by that, Mildew? You're gonna *rescue* me? You gonna save me? You think you can do that?"

And then she pushed through the bushes to where Mildred was standing.

"Well, hello, Stinky. Or is it Slappy?" said the Scarecrow. "I see you've escaped."

"Huh?" Sam blurted. She did not recognize the reassembled Scarecrow right away.

"It's Sam," said Mildred. "She came with us." Mildred looked at her with even more suspicion than she was used to. The lion growled.

"What of it?" Sam raised her chin and looked down at Mildred.

"If you let us, we'll help you get back," said Mildred. Somehow—maybe because she was in Oz or maybe because she was among so many friends—she found that pretty easy to say. There were no bugs in her stomach.

"I don't like you, Mildred. No one likes you. And I don't want your help."

In the background the lion growled low.

"A lot of people like me, Sam, when they get to know me. You should join us now so we can help you get home."

"You guys are gonna lose," she yelled it to the whole crowd. She'd just noticed how they all were standing there, just listening, like they were scared of her. It was going to be easy for the great Mumps to conquer people like this.

She would find a way to do what she came for. The only problem was that the head of the Scarecrow was no longer on the body of the Tin Woodman. Would she have to bring both of them back? And how would she do that—with a lion, even a cowardly one, to protect them? Tin-Puh wanted the body, but the knowledge of their plans was probably in the head of the Scarecrow. Beside the Scarecrow and the Tin Man, the lion crouched. And he growled like an idling engine. The rest of the creatures were further back—a round, brown robot (or was it new kind of Tin Man maybe?), and a four-armed something that seemed to come from a sci-fi movie, and a large eyeless doll who seemed to be offering her a big black button.

Tik-Tok held his everyday blank expression. Everyone else was staring at Sam.

Sam was used to being among people who didn't like her very much. Normally she wasn't too troubled when that happened. She knew there were other people who liked her pretty well or at least found her too useful or too scary to annoy, like the kids who needed her on their kickball team. But here there was a lion and a monster that looked like the kind of giant insect that went on a rampage and ate everyone. She'd be fine as along as she acted confident and made them think she was scary and powerful.

"What do you want?" Louise asked.

"Don't try anything," Sam said. "The Sorceress Mumps, the ruler of the land, protects me."

"From us?" said the Tin Woodman.

"From all danger," she said, "and she has sent me to bring you back to the castle." She pointed at the Scarecrow and the Tin Man. "So come peacefully or she'll send an army."

"Why didn't she send an army to begin with?" the Patchwork Girl asked, her hand still stiffly facing her but her face pointed eerily in the wrong direction.

"I don't like her," said the Wogglebug.

"I don't like her either," said the Tin Woodman. "And for me that is very unusual."

Everyone—except Tik-Tok—took a step toward her. Scraps pulled her second eye out of her pocket and pointed it at Sam. "Yup. That's just where that feeling comes from," she said.

"You *sure* you want to save her?" said Louise. "I doubt her mother would miss her very much."

"No, not really," said Mildred, "but it's the right thing to do."

Sam stepped toward Louise with her arms raised: "You ugly, miserable piece of..." And then the lion roared so loud, no one heard the rest of the sentence. Sam lowered her arms. But she stood tall and faced the lion as though she was afraid of nothing.

"SHE has the ANTI-love magNET," said Tik-Tok.

And everything changed. Every tightened muscle relaxed a little. Scraps unwound her arms. The lion fell back from a roar to an erratic growl. And Mildred and Louise and Thaddeus looked at each other knowingly.

"I thought my heart had stopped working," the Tin Woodman chuckled in relief.

"I still don't like her," said Scraps, "but now that I know why, I can pretend I do."

"WE need the MAGnet back," said Tik-Tok.

"We need it to get home," said Mildred.

"Not necessarily," said Louise.

"But they want to use it to bring back a witch," said Thaddeus. "The Scarecrow said so, and we can't let them do that."

"But that's magic," said Louise, "you don't believe in magic, do you?"

"That's a talking rag doll," said Thaddeus, "and that barrel can swap heads."

Sam put her hand in her pocket and wrapped her fist around the magnet. "Yeah, well, you're not going to get it back. So forget it."

"Why don't you want to go home?" said Mildred.

"When I can join with the Sorceress and take over the whole world?" said Sam.

"Why would you even want to do that?" Mildred asked. "Wouldn't you be better off being happy?"

"Puke," Sam said.

The lion crouched and growled loudly. Sam didn't wait to see if he were going to spring. If she couldn't bring the Tin Man and the Scarecrow with her, she could still get the magnet back to Mumps. Maybe that, along with what she'd learned here, would fix things. She couldn't outrun a lion of course, but the elephant who'd pointed her this way was not far off.

She turned and ran.

The lion stayed crouched, but Mildred took off after her. And seeing that, Louise said something loud, and took off too. And then Thaddeus said the same thing and joined the race.

Sam was fast, almost as fast as Louise. She charged on a straight line toward the castle. And just when she started to slow down and Louise passed Mildred and it looked as though Louise would catch up to her, Sam stopped at the side of the elephant. In a moment the elephant grabbed her in its trunk and flipped her up on its back behind the fur-coated fox.

That was when the Cowardly Lion finally charged out into the open, bursting toward the children. No head start by a human would mean anything to the speed of a lion. But the lion had not counted on the elephant, trumpeting and charging full speed directly at him. In a moment the huge beast reached the children. Then, still trumpeting, it sprinted right past them. And then it reached the lion, who was now standing on his back legs and swiping with his forepaws at the air. But the elephant sprinted past him as well. It charged into the thicket where the others were watching. The children and the lion turned around. Before they could start back after the elephant, it emerged again. The Scarecrow was laid out like a lumpy mattress under the feet of the fox on its back, and the Tin Man was wound up in the elephant's trunk like a pig in a blanket. The huge creature ran with all the speed it had left back to the castle.

By the time the lion had time to react, other elephants, called by the trumpeting of the first, were charging in their direction. The lion sighed.

"What took you so long?" Mildred screamed.

"I was getting up my courage."

"Go get it," said Louise.

But it was too late for that. Several elephants were now running alongside Sam's elephant. And others were charging toward them from a long way off. They ducked back into the thicket.

"We should hide," Thaddeus said. "We're too exposed here. And there's a lot of elephants out there."

They retreated to a place beyond the edge of the cleared forest where the Wogglebug, Tik-Tok and the Patchwork Girl were waiting.

And now there was someone else there too, someone new. And it was the Shaggy Man. He was placing a thick winter coat on the professor's shoulders.

"I hope it fits," he was saying. "I knew you'd be cold. I wasn't sure where to put the extra arms, so I brought some thread to finish it."

"Oh, I could use that," said the Patchwork Girl.

Then the Shaggy Man looked at Mildred, Louise, and Thaddeus. "Come on, American children, coats for all." And he pointed to a wooden wheel barrow laden with coats and firewood and food.

Twenty-One

The Sorceress Lady Mumps said to Tin-Puh, "so how do we use it?" as she grabbed the magnet from Sam. Foxes hauled the Scarecrow and the Tin Woodman into the broken throne room. Tin-Puh clapped his hands and smiled, and Mumps handed the magnet to the Witch Lloco-Monnem.

"Why would you steal an Anti-Love Magnet?" She pointed the tines at the Scarecrow and then at the Tin Man.

The Scarecrow thought for a long time before speaking. He looked at the table where it had lain before he grabbed it. And then he said, "it wasn't yours."

The Witch Lloco-Monnem followed his glance toward the table. The dust from the witch's hat was forming a small cloud over the brim. The dust had acted the same way in her boat when the children were there.

"Oh, by all that's wicked in the world of wicked witches," she said "this was it all along."

"So I'm off the hook, right?" Sam said.

"You did what you were supposed to do," the sorceress said.

Sam glanced at Tin-Puh then at Dox in hope of support. "No whining, Sam." That was what her father always said. And he was right. Whining only made you look weak. And it would probably get her kicked out of the inner circle. The best thing was to get someone else to stand up for you. But no one showed any sign of wanting to do that. She had *not* let the Scarecrow Man escape. She had *not* let the magnet get away. And she *had* risked everything to get it back—all of it and more. But if she pointed all that out, she'd sound whiny. Tin-Puh ought to be especially grateful for the body of the Tin Man. He should defend her. But he didn't seem to even know she was there. Everyone just turned their attention to the next thing. Only the Tin Woodman sighed out of the empty barrel of his chest. But that couldn't be for her.

Well, if what she'd done wasn't enough, she'd just have to do more.

"They're not very nice," the Tin Woodman said, as though he were trying to put that thought into Sam's head. She ignored it. It wasn't about being nice. It was about winning. And Mumps was going to win. She was too great not to win.

Lloco-Monnem pointed the magnet at the hat. Dust rose in a thick little cloud that engulfed the magnet. "I don't know why I didn't see it before," she said, "it's so easy." And she thrust the magnet down the center of the hat. And more dust puffed up and fell back and puffed up bigger. And the sides of the hat seemed to breathe and then groan, getting bigger with every breath until the thread of a seam stretched and nearly burst. And then the seam closed. And then it opened again—and it did explode. Everyone with lungs recoiled in anticipation of a roomful of dust. But that did not happen. The explosion spread a very thin cloud in all directions. And then the cloud drew back to the center, and when it settled, there stood the shriveled form of the Wicked Witch of the West. She was not like the Sorceress Mumps or the Witch Lloco-Monnem. She was no paltry magic worker. She was a genuine witch. She had scraggly hair and a large nose, one bulging eye, and drooping leathery skin all over her body.

"Somebody get me some clothes," she said. "It's cold in here. And a new hat while you're at it. Look what you've done to my hat."

"Oh, great, Wicked Witch," Lloco-Monnem seemed to be on the verge of a long-rehearsed speech.

"Oh, shut up," said the witch.

"But I brought you back to life," Lloco-Monnem said.

"Don't flatter yourself," said the witch.

"Why not?" said Mumps. But no one paid her any attention.

"You restored my body. You didn't bring me back to life. This is Oz. And I'm not sure I'm glad you did it either. Bodies aren't as great as you might think."

"But we are needing..." Tin-Puh began.

"Put your eyes back in your head," the witch walked up to him. "I know what you need. But did it ever occur to you that I might not give it to you? How do you know I'm on your side?"

"You would be on the other side?" said Dox.

"Aren't you getting me clothes, slave?" And Dox went to the door and ordered his foxes to find her some clothes.

"The princess will not like this," said the Scarecrow.

"We could take the clothes off that scarecrow thing," said Mumps.

The Scarecrow and the Tin Woodman were standing along the wall, guarded by two foxes with swords and a hammer.

The witch laughed. "I'd sooner wear that pink abomination you're coated in. Listen, I'm not on anybody's side here. Yes, I could hear everything you said. Rule the world? For what? You want to spend your whole life dodging water buckets, that's your business. As soon as you people fix my castle, you can clear out. If I have to be back in this lumpy body, I'm going to set things back the way they were. Get my Winkies back too. Get my monkeys back if I can. I've had a lot of time to think about this."

Two foxes ran in with an old black dress they'd found in chest in one of the abandoned rooms. The witch slipped it on. It was a little moth-eaten and gave off a faint moldy smell. But all the witch said was, "I seem to be thinner."

"That won't work," said the Tin Woodman, walking away from the wall and the guards. "Ozma has outlawed witches."

"Ozma?"

"Our princess," said the Scarecrow, joining the Tin Woodman in the center of the room.

"You mean they found her?"

The Tin Woodman was about to tell the story when the witch held up her hand, "I guess that changes things." Then she went over to Tin-Puh, "all right, I'll help you get rid of Ozma. The Wizard was not a challenge, but this Ozma could annoy me."

"Hey, I'm in charge here." The Sorceress Mumps rose to her full height and puffed out her chest. The real witch snickered.

"And I'm the queen of the ball," she said. Then she looked at Tin-Puh: "What's the plan?"

"The first thing is to be getting me into that immortal, indestructible tin body," said Tin-Puh.

"That thing?" said the witch, pointing at the tin body.

"Never a worry about overthrow with that beautiful, everlasting armor," he said.

The Witch glanced up and down Tin-Puh and then at the Tin Woodman. "Well, puny thing like you, I guess you won't be losing anything worth having. Yeah, I can do that," she said. "Just need a little time to think it over. Mustn't rush. Lock everybody up until morning. I'll be ready by then."

And then she walked out the door.

"I don't like her very much," said Mumps. "Why do we need her anyway?"

"She has real magic," Tin-Puh said.

"And a deep knowledge of Oz," Lloco-Monnem added. "Once we conquer it, we still have to rule it."

"And the people know her," said Dox.

"Well, I still don't like her. Let's get this over with. What are we waiting for?"

Dox, who had been standing at the window, turned and walked back to the broken throne on which Mumps was sitting. "Nothing at all now. The Emerald City is ready to fall. Tin-Puh has his armor. The Wicked Witch is restored. And we have cleared and burned all but the very last of the growth of the last hundred years around this castle."

"And that matters because?"

"Without wood, we cannot make any more smoke to block the sun and cover the path of the birds across the sky and freeze the Winkies."

Mumps still looked confused. "You promised snow. A real storm."

"The show is being over," said Tin-Puh. "All Oz is being scared. Now we shall do the true work of the conquering. The Emerald City shall be falling tomorrow."

"That was just for show?" said Mumps. "I kind of liked it. Did you see all those cool birds and those colors in the smoke? How did they do the colors?"

"We shall send one last plume of this smoke, one last burst of this cold, one last flock of these birds, you shall rally the foxes and the elephants, and when we are marching on the Emerald City we shall crush it flat underneath the earth. We shall pluck off the leaders and make threats with everyone for doing the same."

"Good. So we don't need the witch, right?"

"We still need the witch," Lloco-Monnem said.

"I don't like her," said the sorceress.

Twenty-Two

Three charging elephants carrying six foxes pushed their forelegs out stiffly as soon as they saw the Shaggy Man. They stopped themselves so abruptly that the foxes nearly flew off their backs.

The Shaggy man was standing, without alarm, as though this were just an ordinary spring morning and he wanted to see what new flowers had emerged. He was just inside the cleared ring of trees, and he was holding up the Love Magnet. All the others stood behind him. They winced at the sight of the braking elephants.

"It would be unkind of you to come any further," the Shaggy Man said. "You should turn around and leave us."

"But," said a fox, recovering from his fright. Before he could finish his sentence, the elephants had already turned around and, shouting back apologies, galloped the foxes back to the castle.

In the clearing, Tik-Tok said it was too late in the day to attack the castle. Orange smoke filled the sky. It was getting dark, and it was getting colder. But the Shaggy Man's coats and his food would satisfy everyone who needed warmth and nourishment, and they could always save Oz in the morning.

The Shaggy Man built a fire, and they all gathered around it.

"It's been pretty hard getting food until now," Thaddeus said, biting into an egg salad sandwich.

"How did you know to come to find us?" the Cowardly Lion asked the Shaggy Man.

"You'd been gone too long. And then these children arrived from America, and I thought they might be in trouble."

"But you said you didn't like us," said Mildred.

"Well that's no reason not to give you food and a warm coat," said the Shaggy Man.

"But that was just the Anti-Love Magnet," said Louise.

"That does explain a lot," said the Shaggy Man, putting an affectionate arm around Louise and Thaddeus and smiling at Mildred. "Sorry about your friend Sam. But as I was saying, it occurred to me that I should have given you the Love Magnet, which can only help in situations like this. So I decided to bring it after all. But then I thought of all the other things American children and a wogglebug might need as well."

"Impeccable ratiocination," said the professor.

"Yeah, I would've been surprised too," said Scraps, "but why did they take the Tin Man and the Scarecrow? That's what I want to know." She was just then laid out across the Shaggy Man's lap, having her eyes sewn back on. "This is going to cost me some fun," she put a floppy hand to her reattached eye button.

"But it will also be the occasion for other fun," said the Shaggy Man.

"scare-CROW was just aBOUT to TELL us WHY he WANTED THE TIN man when the SAM GIRL ar-RIVED," Tik-Tok said.

"Tin-Puh wants his body," said Louise. "He told us that."

"What if he gets it tonight?" said Mildred.

"Then we put it back tomorrow," said the Shaggy Man.

"What if they see our fire?" said Professor Wogglebug.

"Then we invite them to tea," said the Shaggy Man.

"I do not THINK that WOULD WORK."

"But you must remember, we have the Love Magnet." He pulled it out of his shaggy pocket and everyone smiled who could. "It will protect us."

"Perhaps MY THOUGHTS need WINDing but I AM NOT cerTAIN OF that."

"Yeah," said Scraps. "But you're just a clock."

"Which makes him immune to love as well as to anti-love," said the professor, "which would make the idea particularly difficult to absorb."

"Mildred took the Anti-Love Magnet to school, so nobody liked her," Louise said.

"How come we still liked her?" Thaddeus asked.

"Because she's Mildred," said Louise.

"But in the books..." Mildred said.

"I don't think we can trust the books," Louise said, "not very much."

"Really?" said Thaddeus. "But..."

"I know," said Louise. She was petting the mane of the Cowardly Lion. "I still think the books are *mostly* right. But you don't know which parts aren't. So you still have to test everything."

"That's why God gave us brains," Mildred said.

"The Wizard gave the Scarecrow brains," said Scraps.

"I think magic only works here, in Oz," said Thaddeus.

The Shaggy Man chuckled. "Everything worth learning takes time," he said.

"It doesn't matter how long it takes to learn something, as long as you keep trying," said Mildred.

"Oh, I don't know about that," the Patchwork Girl said, moving her head as though she were seeing out of head-placed eyes for the first time. "I learned to like flying the first time I did it. Hey, Lion…"

The Shaggy Man sat the Patchwork Girl up beside him on the fallen tree and got up to tighten Tik-Tok's springs.

"I wonder how Sam is going to treat you when you get back," Thaddeus said, "if we get back, of course, and if you can get her to go back."

"Why would she treat me any different?"

"Because now you'll have this common experience."

"If this is common where you live, I want to go there too," said Scraps.

"Maybe she'll want to be your friend," Louise said. "Wouldn't that be awful."

"But if she changed that much, maybe it wouldn't be awful," Thaddeus said.

"What makes you think we're even getting back," said Mildred. "I don't think the Love Magnet by itself is going to change everything."

"Everyone always gets back," said Louise.

"But you just said…" Mildred smiled.

"Maybe that part's true," Louise said.

"Do you still want to save her, Mildred?" Thaddeus asked.

"It's the right thing to do," Mildred said.

"Well, I don't get that," Louise said.

"You don't help people because they deserve help. You help them because they need help."

"So what you're saying is if she gets back with us, that means she wants to get back with us. And if she wants to get back with us, she will have to have figured out she belongs back there. So that makes it right, right?" Thaddeus said.

"It's just right," said Mildred.

Thaddeus rubbed his arms. "I'm cold again," he said.

"You're cold?" said Louise.

"Well my front is toasty but my back is cold."

From the other side of the campfire, the Wogglebug put a tea cup down with a click on a saucer and made a sigh of pleasure. "Food pills are efficient, but nothing quite satisfies like tea," he said. "Now, I am the kind of Wogglebug that can freeze solid and then thaw out the next day and never hurt at all for the experience. I won't say I enjoy it. But you children may not be so lucky. I suggest you find all the blankets you can and lie as close to the fire as is safe, that you keep the warm fire on the one side of you and the warm lion on the other and call it a night."

"Hey, that's the brightest thing you've ever said today," said the Patchwork Girl. "And being made all out of blankets, I think I know how I can help."

Twenty-Three

Scraps spent the night staring up at the sky with her newly reattached, uncloseable eyes. Things looked new, as though her eyes were new buttons. Or maybe it had just been a long time since she'd stared at the sky so long at night. Clouds floated by. At first the view was so full of stars it looked as though all the thread had been pulled out of a ginormous ream of black cloth, leaving millions of pinholes of different sizes that the light peeked through. There was a ribbon of light to the left that was the Milky Way. And then the clouds came in, and it seemed as though the stars were not pricks of light but dabs of chalk and the Milky Way was where someone had cleaned an eraser by beating it against the sky. But then the clouds were an even bigger eraser, wiping out all the objects from one side of the page to the other in big bunches: the stars, the Milky Way, and the little sliver of the moon in the corner. And then everything was one shade of black. And then, hours later, the clouds put everything back on the canvas, the stars, the moon, the Milky Way, but they were all in different places. That was fun to see.

And then something else moved across the sky, taking out a handful of stars at a time and putting them back immediately and taking more and putting them back. And it was a witch. On her broom, or was it an umbrella, flying circles all over the place.

Scraps jumped up, pointing, and ran to Tik-Tok.

"I see HER," said the copper man.

"Should we wake them up?" Scraps whispered.

"I'm awake," said the Shaggy Man.

"she's COMing," said Tik-Tok.

Like a boulder dropped by the moon, the witch fell out of the sky and landed near their fire, not with a boom but with a swoosh.

Scraps was about to wake the Lion, but the low voice of the witch said, "I only want to talk." They could see her like a standing shadow just outside the circle of light the fire gave off. She was holding her side. She took a step back. The Shaggy Man felt the Love Magnet jump in his deep coat pocket.

"Keep away from me, ragged man," the witch said.

"What do you want?" Scraps asked.

"My, my. What a crazy lot of creatures have come to Oz since I left. I will have to learn more about you. But that's for later. Now, I need to know more about Ozma."

"what IS it YOU WANT to KNOW?" said Tik-Tok.

The witch looked a long time at the copper man. She would have liked to get closer, but stabbing pain in her side grew more and more intense the closer she got to the Shaggy Man. She stayed well away. She said, "What does she think of me?"

"I have never heard her speak of you," said the Shaggy Man.

"I need to talk to her," said the witch. "I want my castle back. I will help you get rid of the invaders if I get my castle back."

"Haven't they promised it to you?" the Shaggy Man said.

"I don't trust them."

"And you find that, mysteriously, you like us," said the Shaggy Man, taking out the Love Magnet and stepping toward her. The witch yelped and stepped away.

"Stay where you are," she said.

The Shaggy Man stepped back.

"Why should I have to like you?" said the witch.

"You have your flying stick," said Scraps. "Go talk to Ozma yourself."

"I don't trust her either," said the witch.

"Tell her what's happening," said the Shaggy Man. "Give her reason to trust you."

"WE could USE HELP from GLIND-a if SHE CAN get it here."

The sky grew just barely perceptibly brighter. The witch's face took on a dark greyness against the black of dress. The witch took a step back. She stood still and quiet as a picture for a long time.

"Tell her you've changed," said the Shaggy Man.

The Cowardly Lion opened his eyes and slowly moved his head. He sniffed. A dusty odor, an old impulse from an ancient memory flooded his brain. Without thinking, he leaped and charged. The nervous witch mounted her umbrella and, faster

than the lion charged, tore off into the sky and was gone.

"Hey," said Scraps, "you sure picked a funny time to have courage."

Twenty-Four

At the first glow of the sun's bright thumbnail over Munchkin Land, thick plumes of dark birds and dark smoke bellowed up one last time into the sky and spread in all directions. The rambunctious cacophony of caws and shrieks woke every fox and every elephant in the delipidated castle. For the first time in many weeks, they did not go to harvest trees. The last of the trees was just then being burned in the furnace to make the last smoke for the birds to blow with their turbulent wings, terrorizing the Land of the Winkies. In the midst of this grating uproar, Tin-Puh turned the key on the broken door and, with Sam behind him, entered the room where the Tin Woodman and the Scarecrow were imprisoned. There were fox guards stationed just outside. They'd been there all night with torches and hammers.

"Things are a little different today, aren't they Scarecrow?" Sam shouted above the din.

Tin-Puh held up a hand to silence her, and he smiled and politely bowed as he waited for the clamor to end. The Scarecrow and the Tin Man looked at each other, then they looked up at the rising flock and blowing smoke—which seemed perhaps a little thinner to the Scarecrow than it had seemed the day before. Tin-Puh put his hands over his ears in a gesture that didn't seem to be protective but rather to convey the idea "isn't it loud in here?"

When the flutter died down, he smiled broadly and said to the Tin Man, "I am knowing you are knowing why I come. But I must to say part of me does regret losing such wonderful specimen of iron rule, but weak must to give way to strong. It is world's way."

"It's tin rule, really," said the Tin Man.

Sam laughed. Tin-Puh held up his gloved hand to silence her.

"As long as he can keep the head, we can always find the tinsmith to make him another body," said the Scarecrow.

"But I would once again be without a heart," said the Tin Woodman. "And tin is plentiful, but hearts are very hard to find."

"Perhaps we can ask the tinsmith to make you a new tin body of your own," said the Scarecrow to Tin-Puh. "Then you would not need this one."

Tin-Puh paused, and he really seemed to be thinking it over.

"You're not seriously..." Sam began. But she was interrupted

"It is true I need no hearts," Tin-Puh said. "But there is no time for finding this tinsmith. To be loved is useful, to love is not. No, I have body here before me which is everything I am needing. Why I would waste time searching your tinsmith? And when I am putting it on, I am knowing all it knows. You are legendary ruler. And I shall be knowing your secrets. And I shall be immortal and impervious. It shall be done. It must be done. As is concerning the heart, I shall tell witch to pull that. I fear it only makes trouble for ruling."

"Where is the Wicked Witch?" asked the Scarecrow.

"On her broomstick, flying with the birds," said Sam. "She's been gone all night."

"She inspects castle," Tin-Puh said as though Sam hadn't spoken.

"And you're going to repair this castle for her?" said the Scarecrow.

"This is her price. We pay it as long as her services shall be useful. But we don't talk of this now. I must to know, in case not everything comes to me with body, how you do it? How maintain extraordinary control to your people?"

"I don't understand," the Tin Man said.

"Your Winkies do all you ask, no questions. There are not war, not bickering between them. Wars maybe are fun, but very expensive. You have not prisons, not executions, and yet when witch needs army to guard this fortress, your Winkies come with sharp weapons and are protecting her. You see I do my research. I need this kind of control."

"I thought the Sorceress Mumps was going to take over," said the Scarecrow.

Tin-Puh chuckled. "You are joking, no?"

"But she is," said Sam.

"You have met her?" Tin-Puh said. "Who would let this be?"

"That's what you said," said the Scarecrow. "First the witch as a puppet, then Mumps as the true ruler." He saw nothing funny.

Tin-Puh chuckled again. "And I was thinking that your pin brains were best in Oz. I was thinking I might even be taking them myself for this head, but mine prove much better. You think we let Mumps rule Oz? She cannot rule bathroom, this blob of gelatin."

"What?" said Sam. He had to know she would tell Mumps of his betrayal. It would be all she needed to win back all of Mumps' affection. The hope made her believe for a moment he was telling the truth. But she was not so easily fooled. No, she could not be that lucky. She understood: Tin-Puh was loyal. He was just blowing smoke to confuse the Scarecrow. Best not to say anything to anyone.

"I don't mind telling you this," Tin-Puh told the Scarecrow, "we pass time till this witch comes."

Tin-Puh stepped around the back of the Tin Woodman and put his hands on his shoulder and elbow like a doctor examining a patient. "I don't mind telling you this, as I am saying, because there shall be nothing you can do, and if you are telling her as I say, I shall but deny, and she shall believe me. She makes good face for some people, like little girl here, who must to learn better if she is to be useful. Mumps tells those people what they wish to be hearing. This is why they are loving her. And they give to her their power like little shiny things. We are keeping her as long as she is useful."

"That's not true," said Sam.

"But she seems so powerful," said the Scarecrow.

"You must to sharpen those pins," Tin-Puh smiled.

"But the Sorceress is beautiful, and she knows everything," Sam said.

The Scarecrow adjusted the sack of his head as though to rearrange the pins inside for better thinking.

"And that is all of that," Tin-Puh said, coming back to the front of the Tin Man, apparently satisfied. "So please to get back to subject of importance. How you do it, Tin Woodman? I shall have to enslave these Winkies."

"The witch enchanted them before I ever was named Emperor."

"Oh?"

"You should have read the books and not the summaries," said the Scarecrow.

"I rule by love," said the Tin Man.

Sam laughed.

"I would never enslave," said the Tin Man.

"So the heart is useless, just as I am thinking. We will not have such problems when we remove it," said Tin-Puh.

"But the heart is everything. I could not rule without it."

"You cannot be tricking me this way. You are not needing hearts. Hearts make you weak."

"You should tell the truth," said Sam.

"But I don't worry about that," said the Tin Man. "I love the Winkies. I do what is best for them."

Tin-Puh paced the room and kicked the pile of dirty straw. "You are not telling me what I must to know. You are telling me what you wish for me to be believing. Yes, you are hoping I shall believe this. But this is what I must to expect from great leader. Yes, it is not much useful for me. I am not this gullible. But no matter. I shall be knowing what is the truth when I am having the body." And then he looked up and pointed at the sky. And there was the witch on her umbrella circling in for a landing.

"I've been doing some looking around," she said in a cloudy voice as soon as she was down. She greeted no one and looked only at Tin-Puh. "Things are not as bad as I feared. The walls are strong except for a few crumbling places in rooms like this. They won't be easy to fix. But it should not take forever. The magic that built them is even better than I expected."

"Are you seeing any other things in your flying?" Tin-Puh asked.

"Nothing remarkable," said the witch.

"You did not to see the band of the enemies by the fire?"

The witch cackled. "As I said, nothing remarkable. A small group with no magic and no weapons. We don't need to worry about them."

"True. We let them come. But they do have weapon. One has powerful weapon among them. I have heard this from foxes," Tin-Puh said.

"They have no weapons at all," said the Tin Man.

"Only the Love Magnet," said the Scarecrow, "and that's not a weapon."

"But this is weapon," said Tin-Puh. "Why be lying about it? This is the day, and this weapon now makes everything as everything must to be. Everything is helping us. It cannot be more perfect."

"Huh?" said Sam. "But it's just a magnet."

"You are not seeing this? None of you is seeing this? You see why I need no heart, man of tin. I am not wishing to love. I need not to love. I need just only being loved. People shall love me, and I shall enslave them. And then I am not even needing love from them." He turned to the Witch, "Soon as the people love us, they shall abandon the sorceress. She sees their love for her is shallow as her own. We need not the unstable sorceress after that. But we must to get started," said Tin-Puh.

"I hadn't thought of that," said the witch.

Tin-Puh opened the door and let the guards in. One of them held the Scarecrow back while Sam and two more helped Tin-Puh and the witch perform the operation to transform him from Tin-Puh into Tinman-Puh. It did not take long. The witch worked quietly and deliberately. She took off the tin head and tossed it to one of the foxes guarding the Scarecrow. He dropped it on the floor at the Scarecrow's feet. She opened a little door in the chest and pulled the Tin Man's heart out and handed it to Sam. Sam threw it where the head had gone. The Scarecrow caught it and stuffed it in his pocket.

Finally with the help of the guards, she tossed Tin-Puh's former body over the side of the castle for the ravens to find, and then she was done. Tinman-Puh moved his arms and kicked his new legs.

"Everything is working, I hope," the Wicked Witch said.

Tinman-Puh swiveled his head.

"Oh, don't try to turn it too fast or too far," said the witch.

"It is feeling loose," he said.

"It will need to grow into place. It'll take a few days. Just be careful with it a while. No activity for a week or so. Best if you stay in bed."

Tinman-Puh stared back in deep concern. "There is not time for this. I tell you already, this is the day."

"Oh, I don't think so," said the witch. "The head could fall right off."

Tinman-Puh huffed. "This should have been said before." His voice was angry and threatening.

The witch rubbed the back of her neck. "Well, you do what you like. I did my part." She pointed a crooked finger at his new tin chest. "If you don't need my help anymore, you just let me know. And remember, I have the antidote. That Love Magnet will not work on me."

Still agitated, Tinman-Puh tried to sound less threatening. "We go today. If head fall off, you shall put head back on." He moved the head slowly back and forth. "Is good fit. I rule with metal. I never die."

Twenty-Five

The Patchwork Girl poked her colorful head through a green bush. The field was empty. Not an elephant or fox to be seen. It felt like an ordinary morning in Oz.

And that felt weird. What did it mean?

"WE shall FIND out."

"But we're going to be careful, anyway, I suppose," said Scraps, "but what I want to know is, what was with that Wicked Winkie West Witch anyway?"

The Shaggy Man told everyone about the witch's nighttime visit. "I think she was going to offer to help us."

"Yeah, before doughty-head here scared her off," said Scraps.

"I don't think we should trust wicked witches," said Louise.

"Oh, I don't know," said the professor. He had done some research on Wicked Witches. "It may be possible we have misunderstood her."

"I don't think so," said Louise.

"How would *you* know either way?" asked the Wogglebug. "You're not from Oz."

"I have read the books," Louise said, "all of them: Baum, Plumly, Neil, Snow…"

"She trapped me," said the Cowardly Lion. "I was imprisoned a long time in that horrible castle."

"I'm not saying she's nice," said the professor, "but she captured you because you were out to destroy her, right?"

"Actually, she captured him just because he was in her territory," said Louise.

"My research is different," said the professor. "The truth is, what she has always wanted is just what she said she wanted last night: to be left alone. I think…"

"But that's not true," said Louise.

"Yeah, but the books…" said Thaddeus.

"She enslaved everyone she couldn't kill," said Louise.

"Once, again," said the Wogglebug, "I'm not saying she's nice."

"I don't think this is going to help us," said Mildred.

"Oh, boy, there's gonna be a lot to talk about later, ain't there?" said the Patchwork Girl. "But what do we do now?"

She addressed the question to Tik-Tok, who had been shifting his weight from one foot to another and making loud mechanical noises for several seconds.

"THERE is noWHERE to HIDE BEtween here AND the castle," he said. "IF it IS A trap, IT is A TRAP. WE STILL have to GO."

Meanwhile in the castle, Tinman-Puh and the Wicked Witch were advancing toward the throne room. Sam was walking behind them.

"Remember, your head is still loose," said the witch, "perhaps it would be good if you explained the plan. There may be some magic to help hold the head in place if I know exactly what your plan is."

"We have said. We gather foxes and elephants and we march upon this Emerald City. When this Love Magnet arrives, we are taking it. Before we are arriving to city, it is already fallen. And now we are having this magnet, nobody to resist. Is easy."

"So it's just riding elephants?" said Sam.

"*If* you can get the magnet," said the witch. "But I was asking about my castle. What is the plan for fixing the walls and the roof and the supports of my castle?"

"As soon as Oz is won."

"I don't like it," she said.

"I think we have to give the weapon to the sorceress," Sam said.

"You are not consulted," Tinman-Puh said.

"Don't waste my help," said Sam. "And just so you know, the sorceress doesn't even need a love magnet. We will do whatever she asks."

Tinman-Puh raised his new tin hand to his fleshy chin and rubbed it, and said nothing.

"So what is the rest of the plan?" Sam put an edge of irritation in her voice. "What do we do when we're actually in the city?"

Tinman-Puh stopped and turned and stared hard at Sam. She stared right back.

"How can I help you if I don't know your plan? I know you don't believe what you said to the Scarecrow. You saw how *I* got the Scarecrow and Tin Man and how *I* got the magnet back. I am very good at this." She clenched her teeth.

The witch watched.

From the superior height of the Tin Man's body, Tinman-Puh stared down. When he spoke, he spoke very slowly: "You will be staying out of the way. And you will doing as you are told, or you will be being locked up with your friends."

"Listen," Sam said. But she could not say any more. Tinman-Puh placed the palm of his hand over her nose and mouth and

spread his fingers as far as they would go across her face and pushed her head into the wall and held her there. Rivets on the cold metal hands dug deep into the soft flesh of her cheek over the bone. She was afraid her nose would break. And then she was afraid of much worse. She did not struggle.

"And you shall say no more to me again unless I first speak to you. I do not ask you 'is this clear?' If you are opening your mouth again, you shall be prisoner before you finish first word."

Tinman-Puh dropped his hand away. Sam had to fight against sinking to the floor. She had to push down rising tears. She put her two hands to her face, afraid even to whimper. Tinman-Puh turned calmly to the Wicked Witch. "We have made fear far and wide as can be made with our smoke and our birds. Emerald City is falling today. The great weapon comes to us unasked and just now, at right time. Now is this moment. No more waiting. Soon as we have Oz, we shall have all the prisoners we need to fix this little castle."

The witch bit her lip so she would not laugh.

A young fox ran up to announce that the invading force was advancing just outside the castle.

"This is what you do," said Tinman-Puh to the fox, "you take overwhelming force, and you grab all. This witch goes with you."

"You sure you want me to do that?" said the witch.

He stared at her. She did not blink or look away.

"You are only one." Tinman-Puh looked back at the messenger fox. "One of them has weapon must be captured. He holds it up when he sees you. This Wicked Witch shall go to him, slow. His weapon is made useless by closeness to her. This I think. That is magic of it. You are easy to take weapon from him. Then you have it, you bring it to me in throne room. The rest shall give you no trouble."

The Wicked Witch scratched her chin with her long fingernails. She left with the messenger.

Tinman-Puh called after her, "Head stays on good. No problem."

In a moment he was alone with Sam.

Tin-Puh's own body had been short and a little plump, and Sam had had no reason to think she should fear anything it could do. But Tinman-Puh was taller and stronger. Sam had never felt fear before, not of anything or anyone. She could handle pain. In the past, whenever she resisted force or rules—which she never did recklessly but always with confidence and calculation as her father had taught her—she always got her way. Persistence and strength and fearlessness, it was a combination she thought nothing could defeat. Now she knew she was wrong. Tin-Puh had had persistence and fearlessness in equal measure. And now, as Tinman-Puh, he had greater strength. She walked behind him in silence.

Twenty-Six

The door at the base of the mountain was unlocked and unguarded. It opened easily. No one made a sound as the door swung open. The copper man stepped in and looked around. A staircase faced him a few paces in. The hall was quiet and empty.

"Perhaps they cleared out when they saw us coming?" said Scraps.

"I don't like it," said the Wogglebug. "I'd prefer to talk in the open."

"But we have the Love Magnet," said Mildred.

"And this is Oz," said Louise.

"But Tin-Puh, he's not from Oz. And this Sorceress the Scarecrow told us about, where is she from?"

"No, no. This is Oz and we do have the Magnet. So, if Tik-Tok approves, I will go first," said the Shaggy Man. "And if we meet anyone, they will love me and let me pass."

Tik-Tok backed out to take up the rear with the Wogglebug. The Shaggy Man entered, and everyone followed. At first, the stairs were dark, but then Louise took out her phone.

She turned on the flashlight, to the delight of Scraps. But it wasn't very helpful. The stairway was still dark past the edge of the light until they came to a small opening on one side. Louise stuck her phone in.

A hundred pairs of fox eyes and elephant eyes stared back. At the same moment the door through which they'd entered slammed shut behind them and a loud voice called for them to stop.

"Run," yelled Thaddeus.

"No need to run," the Shaggy Man said calmly. But the children were already in flight. They squeezed past the Shaggy Man and took off up the stairs.

"Unforeseen complication," said the Wogglebug.

The stairway wound up past closed doors until it let out in the bottom floor of the castle proper.

"We really should have waited for the others," Thaddeus said, half out of breath.

"They didn't follow us?" said Louise.

"Didn't you hear the Shaggy Man?" said Mildred.

"No," said Louise.

"He said we didn't have to run," said Mildred.

"Then why did you run?" said Louise.

"Because you ran," said Mildred.

"Let's go back," said Thaddeus.

The furry shadow of a fox darted behind them and blocked the stairway. An open window in front of them let in light. From the left and right, hallways stretched that were fast filling with foxes.

One short fox who approached, walking on his hind legs, yanked Louise's phone out of her hand. "So this must be the weapon."

"Hey," Louise swiped for the phone, but the fox pulled it back.

And then a short, wrinkled woman in a black dress stood before them. She took the phone, glanced at it quickly, then threw it out the window. "That's not the weapon," she said. "Hold these until the others arrive."

Up the stairs, pushed by a column of foxes, came all the rest.

The whole company crowded into the room at the top of the stairs.

"Hello, my friends," said the Shaggy Man, pulling the Love Magnet from his coat and holding it between his fingers.

"That's the weapon," said the witch, grabbing her stomach and slowly approaching. "Take it."

"I'm sure you'd rather move aside and let us pass," said the Shaggy Man. And the fox smiled and gave the strangers room to pass up the stairs.

"Take it," yelled the witch, holding her side tighter with both hands and stepping closer. A look of pain came over her face. "Take it, now."

"You should bring us to see the sorceress," said the Shaggy Man.

And the fox in front of him reached out his forepaw and said, "Hand it over."

The Shaggy Man waved the magnet as though to free the power.

The witch closed her eyes and contorted her face and pulled hard at her side. "Just take it," she groaned.

A look of profound confusion fell over the Shaggy Man's face, as profound as the look of pain on the face of the witch. No one here seemed to be at all affected by the power of the Love Magnet, which had never failed before.

An old fox from out of nowhere leaped at the Shaggy Man and grabbed the Love Magnet in her teeth and charged past the witch up the stairs.

The witch exhaled a great sigh of relief.

"What I wouldn't give for a glass of water," said the Lion.

Twenty-Seven

Lloco-Monnem and King Dox were leading a sleepy Sorceress Mumps to her broken throne when a fox rushed in, running on all fours, with the Love Magnet in her teeth.

"What a nice little fox," said the Sorceress. "Why do we always do things so early in the day?"

"It's nearly noon," said Lloco-Monnem.

"You're an obnoxious woman, you know that," the Sorceress said. "But that's a nice little fox."

Tinman-Puh pulled the magnet from the fox's mouth and, smiling broadly, held it tight. He ordered the loyal messenger to join the masses of foxes and elephants gathering in the courtyard outside the window.

"What is it?" the sorceress asked. "Hey, you wearing a new suit?"

"Is all we need to finish conquest. This weapon of weapons," Tinman-Puh said.

"It makes everyone who sees you love you," said Lloco-Monnem.

"Hah," said the Sorceress. "What a waste. Everyone already loves me."

"Ah, that's not quite true," said the Witch Lloco-Monnem. "You have enemies."

"Losers don't count."

"The people of Emerald City shall accept you much more gladly when you shall be marching Emerald Streets with this in pocket," said Tinman-Puh.

"Let's at least get it gold-plated first."

"You also might want to have it at hand when you address your foxes and elephants," Dox added. "They've been working very hard."

"When does that happen?"

"They gather right now," said Tinman-Puh. "We have speech right here." He glanced over at the fox king. "Dox, give him speech."

The Fox King pulled a sheaf of papers from his waistcoat.

"*Read?* No, don't think so. I don't need your speech and I don't need a filthy Love Magnet. I have the best words. Don't you worry."

"She's very tired," said Lloco-Monnem.

"What shall you be telling them?" Dox asked.

"Great stuff. Stuff no one's ever heard before. Wonderful job. Making Oz marvelous, you know, again, for the first time ever. How we've cleared away the smoke and warmed the nasty little place, and how those disgusting little Oz birds are returning."

Tinman-Puh walked up to the sorceress, which made her smile, something no one had ever seen before. Teeth like broken shards of porcelain plates or like a shifting row of old marble tombstones rose up and down the hills of her massive mouth. "You're the only foreigner I ever liked," she said. "I'm actually a Gillikin, you know. Never told anyone that. It's why I like purple so much. Is that the Tin Man's suit? You finally got it."

"Yes," said Tinman-Puh, putting a hand on the Sorceress's back and leading her to the window.

The sorceress looked down on a growing crowd of foxes and elephants flowing like water into the walled, stone courtyard, filling the space between the lower ramparts and the high tower. Everything was orange and grey. Foxes like long orange snakes slithered up and over and around; they threaded themselves through the legs of the elephants as they settled into place, finally perching on the elephant's big backs by the dozen, sitting and nipping like dogs. The courtyard filled almost to bursting, filled and filled until there was no room for any more.

At the sight of the pink robe and free-flowing, fox-colored, cotton-candy hair of the sorceress, cheers broke upward like a strong wind. Tinman-Puh dropped the Love Magnet into the Sorceress Lady Mumps's wide, sheer pocket.

"What did I tell you?" Mumps barked at Tinman-Puh. "They love me. Now back up. I have a speech to deliver."

Twenty-Eight

After locking the prisoners in a room more secure than the one Sam had escaped from, the fox guards, not wanting to miss a word of the sorceress's speech, ran to the courtyard.

"What happened?" asked Scraps. "We had the love magnet."

"They had the Anti-Love Magnet," said Thaddeus.

"We should have thrown it in the river," said Louise.

Mildred couldn't think of anything to say.

"How we gonna get out of this pickle?" said Scraps.

Escape seemed impossible, until the Wicked Witch knocked on the door.

"Are you going to let us out?" said Scraps.

"Will I get my castle back? Will I be left in peace?"

For several seconds, no one said anything.

"Tell her 'yes,'" said Thaddeus.

But what Tik-Tok said was, "THAT will BE UP to OZma."

"At least I know you're not lying. Sadly, I don't have a key. This could take a while."

Scraps grabbed a key from Tik-Tok's side, and slid it under the door. Several seconds passed. Then came the sound of the tumblers turning in the lock. Opening the door, they found the key still in the lock, but the witch was nowhere to be seen.

"You see," said the Wogglebug. "She may not be quite the evil she was reported to be."

"She caught us, she stole the Love Magnet, she had us locked away in this room, and then she let us out. Does anyone else here think this witch is cockoo?" said Scraps.

"WE must BE CAREful," said Tik-Tok. "But WE HAVE TO do what we HAVE to DO."

The Scarecrow led the way to the throne room. Once there, he held the Tin Head in front of the door just far enough for him to peer inside.

Twenty-Nine

Looking up from the courtyard stuffed with elephants and foxes, Sam watched the Sorceress Mumps advance to the window and raise herself high: she threw back her shoulders, pulled back her chin, and snorted. Looking up from the branches of a tree, the only tree in the courtyard, a dead apple tree, Sam was filled with love.

Up above, raising herself on a box to reach an impressive height, Mumps seemed to float into position. She held out her hand to quiet and ready the crowd. Then she paused a long time. Her orange, candy hair and her gauzy, pink robe fluttered in little eddies of wind. Her face had a tangerine glow—the most beautiful thing Sam had ever seen.

The only mar in the picture was the sight of Tinman-Puh standing beside the beloved lady, tall in the Tin Man's body, whispering in her ear.

And then the Sorceress Lady Mumps held out her hand to quiet the crowd.

Through the courtyard door, down from the stairs that led up to the throne room, stepped the shriveled old witch, carrying an umbrella. Seeing all the elephants, she hopped onto the umbrella and flew over their heads to Sam's dead tree, taking up a branch on the other side of the trunk. Sam looked at her with suspicion. The witch cackled.

"You're not supposed to like me," she said. "But now that I have this thing inside me, I don't have to worry anymore that you might."

"Okay," Sam replied. She didn't want to talk to the shriveled witch anyway. She wanted to be up there with Mumps. She did not want to be in this courtyard among the press of elephants and ordinary foxes. They smelled, and they chomped on cookies and peanuts and gabbed among themselves so that it was hard to make out what Mumps was saying. Now and then they grew so loud, nattering and trumpeting, that Sam couldn't hear the Sorceress at all. But she'd been ordered to the courtyard by Tinman-Puh. And she understood that he would stop at nothing to keep her away from Mumps. And although she was already planning how to get around that, for the time being, it was safer to go where she was told.

"But you don't have to like me to work with me," said the witch.

"I'll think about it," Sam said. But all she was thinking about at that moment was Mumps.

"I can help you defeat Tin-Puh," said the witch.

"What are you?" a fox called up at Sam from the back of an elephant.

"I just want to hear the Sorceress," Sam said.

"What's with the accent," said the elephant. "You're not from Oz, are you?"

"Are *you?*" said Sam.

"We're from the general area," said the fox.

"All of Oz will be part of Foxville very soon," another fox added with a snarl.

"These silly animals will be our slaves once Tin-Puh and Lloco-Monnem are gone," the witch whispered so only Sam could hear.

Tinman-Puh glared down at the crowd and seemed to pick out Sam specifically and challenge her with just his eyes. She felt an impulse to look away. But she didn't. She stared back for a moment, then turned her eyes to the sorceress and, without moving them away, spoke to the elephant at the foot of her tree.

"I'm worried," she said. "I think the sorceress is being manipulated by that Tin-Puh."

"They aren't worth your breath," said the witch. "Let them talk."

"No one manipulates Mumps," said the elephant. "She's got a mind like six elephants. She's got a plan."

"I was there. Look up, he's right beside Mumps. He's feeding her what to say," Sam said to any fox or elephant that would listen.

"They won't help you defeat Tin-Puh," said the witch. "You need me for that."

"So you're one of them, then," said a third fox. "You want to just hand Oz over to that usurper, Ozma. How'd you even get in here?"

"I saw it," Sam told them. "Tin-Puh wants to take over. He's trying to use her. And then he's going to steal the weapon and... and..."

"Quiet," trumpeted an elephant. "She said something about marching on the Emerald City." And then the elephant trumpeted loud enough for all the elephants and foxes to hear: "We're attacking the Emerald City."

And then the scene in the great window changed. Funny things started to happen. Tinman-Puh raised his right hand and held it out in front of him. Then he backed away from the window with a curious shout. Then he disappeared. The sorceress kept talking. The crowd below went silent and as the noise of shouting come from the window. Dox and a handful of fox guards appeared and disappeared in the frame. Then Tinman-Puh was back at the window and he raised his left hand to his flap-eared, funnel hat and lifted it off his head, and threw it into the crowd. Why would he do that? More shouting. A puzzled expression bloomed on Tinman-Puh's face. It did not seem to be the appropriate gesture to go with the words he shouted at everyone watching: "Are we ready?"

"Something's wrong," said the witch. And she stood on the branch and gathered in her umbrella.

"Are you going up there?" Sam asked without thinking. "Take me."

"Take the stairs," she said.

Sam scrambled down the tree. All the elephants pounded the ground. Pound, pound, pound. It felt like an earthquake. And then there was a real jolt. A crack ran through the pavement of the courtyard. More cracks formed in every direction. The stone tiles of the floor fractured all over its surface. Sam's tree shook hard. For a second, she was afraid it was a real earthquake.

But the elephants' stomping stopped. And everything got quiet.

Sam ran to the door and took off up the cracked stairs.

Thirty

No one noticed the Tin Head, held in the Scarecrow's hands, peering into the room through the doorway.

"I think this will work," said the Tin Head.

"Do you see the magnet?" Mildred asked.

"It's in the fat lady's pocket."

At the window Lady Mumps shouted down, "My foxes, my elephants, our work is done. At this very minute, the last columns holding up the Emerald City are being pulled out. A great earthquake has begun. Towers are falling. And the whole city is crashing into the ground."

"Oh, dear," said Scraps.

"Everything that falls can be fixed," the Shaggy Man whispered. "First, get the magnet."

The magnet lay heavy in Mumps' lace pocket. Now that he could see his body, the Tin Woodman felt he could probably make it move anywhere he wanted it to go. To prove it, he sent Tinman-Puh running a funny little circle around the room. Then he sent him to the window and made him throw his hat into the crowd. The eyes on the Puh-head snapped open, big as bullseyes on a target. He shouted something out the window. Scraps would have laughed if she'd seen it. And he made funny sounds as though he were riding a kicking horse. Everyone in the room started running in circles and making loud noises.

When the Tin Head saw how easy it was to move his body, he sent it to the Sorceress and made it grab the magnet and tear the pocket from the robe.

Mumps shrieked. But she kept talking.

That was when things stopped being easy. At first, Tinman-Puh had been too surprised to resist. But when he felt himself tear Mumps' pocket out of her robe, that changed. At the sound of Mumps' piglet-shriek, Dox burst into action. The fox king grabbed for the magnet. A loud gasp rose from the courtyard. Just as he got hold of the tin hand that held the magnet, the king was sent flying with a swing of the Tin Man's arm. The magnet sailed across the room. Tinman-Puh pushed his body toward the lost weapon. The Tin-Head pulled against him to keep him away.

Then the Wicked Witch on her umbrella appeared at the window. But she grabbed her side and would not come through it into the room. Mumps swatted at her like a fly.

"You're ruining my speech," the sorceress cried. "Someone get her out of here."

The ground had started to rumble again, a little earthquake.

Lloco-Monnem in confusion grabbed the window ledge. She was too close to Mumps to see past her bulk to what was going on on the other side of the room. When the Wicked Witch yelled at her to get the magnet, she did not know where it was. The Wicked Witch flew to the other side of the wide, open window and screamed at

Dox to get up. But he'd been thrown too hard into the wall and was dazed.

Just then Sam appeared in the doorway. She saw the Scarecrow holding the head of the Tin Woodman.

"Hello, Samantha," said the Shaggy Man.

Sam stopped in her tracks. Mildred was standing beside the Shaggy Man. And there were Louise and Thaddeus. And there was the Tin Head peering in the doorway.

"Hi," she said to the Shaggy Man. "But…" There was so much confusion in the room, so much rumbling in the building. Rocks were falling from the top of the walls.

"We could use your help," said the Shaggy Man.

"You're with Mildred?" She made a face.

"Oz is in trouble," said the Shaggy Man.

"Help us, Sam," said Mildred.

"But, Mumps…" Then she reared back. She said, "no," and kicked the Tin Woodman's head from between the hands of the scarecrow like a football player scoring an extra point. And then she darted into the melee.

"That is certainly disappointing," the Shaggy Man said.

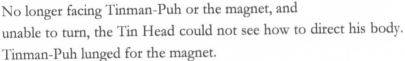

The Tin Man's head flew toward the large opening of the window. It would have flown clear out into the courtyard if Mumps herself had not been standing smack in the way. The head bounced off her soft belly and rattled to the floor. No longer facing Tinman-Puh or the magnet, and unable to turn, the Tin Head could not see how to direct his body. Tinman-Puh lunged for the magnet.

The floor was unsteady. The rotten roof was raining down in pieces. But the loudest sound was the tearful crying of Mumps, holding her side where the Tin Man's head had hit her. She was stomping her feet and screaming, "My speech, my speech. Oh, oh, my side, my pocket. My favorite robe."

Sam saw what Tinman-Puh was lunging for and threw herself at the magnet. At the same moment, Mildred saw the magnet and Sam. She yelled, "stop her," as she too lunged for the magnet. But Sam was a step ahead of her. And Tinman-Puh was even closer. Louise and Thaddeus charged in after Mildred. Louise outran Sam, and grabbed her by the belt. Thaddeus headed for Tinman-Puh. He pushed hard at the tin barrel of his belly and threw him back onto the shaking floor. His Puh head came off from the force and rolled to the wall.

Mildred grabbed the magnet.

Down in the courtyard all the foxes and elephants were in a panic from the rumbling ground and the strange scene they were watching in the window. The elephants were stomping so hard, no one realized that the ground had again stopped quaking.

Sam threw Louise off her and lunged for Mildred. Mildred stood her ground, and gripped tightly the Love Magnet.

"Oh, you're not so bad," said Sam, stopping.

Lloco-Monnem understood what was happening. She took a step toward the magnet—but then she stopped. She smiled a hideous smile. For several seconds, the only sound was the blubbering of the Sorceress Lady Mumps.

"My castle," yelled the Wicked Witch, still hovering just outside the window. Groaning in pain, but immune to the Love Magnet, she darted into the room. Mildred saw her coming and pointed the Love

Magnet directly at her. The witch sailed directly at her. Mildred felt a strong tug on the Love Magnet. She gritted her teeth and held on tight.

The witch screamed in pain. With a puff of dust, the Anti-Love Magnet shifted in the witch's stomach and flew from her side. Mildred fell back. The Anti-Love Magnet careened past her and smacked into the wall by the entrance and fell to the floor. The Shaggy Man stepped on it and held it down.

The Wicked Witch, still groaning, turned her umbrella around and screamed out the window and was gone.

For the third time, the castle and the mountain on which it stood began to tremble.

The Scarecrow, the Lion, Scraps, Tik-Tok, and the Wogglebug stepped into the room. The Scarecrow ran to the Tin Woodman's head, and picked it up gently. Scraps ran to Tin-Puh's head and grabbed it by the ears and stared into its eyes and said, "oops." Then she tossed it like a piece of trash out the window into the crowd of chaotic elephants and foxes.

"What's going on?" yelled a fox below, holding out his arms to steady himself on the shaky ground.

And down sailed the head.

The rumbling of the ground moved like waves across the courtyard. The wall at the edge of the courtyard split and crumbled and cascaded down the mountain.

A fox reached out to catch Tin-Puh's soaring head, but the shifting ground made her miss. The head bounced off the backside of an elephant and went hurtling down the side of the mountain like an avalanching rock.

The rumbling of the earthquake grew and grew.

The frame around the big window cracked and broke, and the whole mountain on which the castle stood bumped and slid several feet down into the earth. Mumps fell backward into the room.

When it seemed as though the whole castle would tumble down upon them, the shaking stopped again. The ground grew calm. But everything upon it was commotion. Fearing the total collapse of the mountain as well as the castle, all the foxes in the courtyard raced down the rocky slope as fast as they could go, leaving the elephants, who could not climb down the steep mountain, stampeding for the narrow, shaky stairs.

In the castle, the broken throne room caved in as more of the ceiling and crumbling walls came bounding down in pieces. Mildred dodged a falling shingle but then was thrown onto her back by the quaking floor. Bracing herself, she lost the Love Magnet, which went flying. Sam pushed Thaddeus aside with one hand and Louise with the other and caught it like a lazy fly ball and smiled just as the shaking stopped.

The damaged castle did not fall, and although the mountain sank, the magic that had created it still held. The building cracked and lost many stones. But it did not collapse.

The Sorceress Lady Mumps sat on floor, blubbering. But now she looked over at Sam, and she smiled. All around Sam, everyone was smiling. Witch Lloco-Monnem came up to her and said, "You have the weapon. Dox," she turned around to urge the fox king to join her, "she has the weapon. We will win yet."

"Samantha," the Shaggy Man called to her from where he stood by the doorway. "I hope you will be good enough to return my Love Magnet."

Under his foot he felt a strong vibration.

Sam stared at Shaggy man, then looked the other way, at the weeping Mumps. She didn't say anything to the Shaggy Man. She didn't know what to say. She turned all her attention on Mumps. She walked over and knelt down and showed her the Love Magnet. "Why are you crying? We won."

"Maybe we don't need her," Lloco-Monnem whispered. "Maybe just you and me, and Dox—if you want him."

"Maybe just me and her," said Sam. She helped Mumps to her feet, an injured, fallen, helpless old lady, and walked her over to her broken throne. Everyone just watched. She sat her down on the chair. And then she handed her the magnet.

"I am loyal," she said. "Don't cry."

"My robe," she said. "He ripped it. Tin-Puh tore the pocket." And she put her hand in the hole where the pocket had been torn to get the magnet out. "My very favoritest robe."

Sam felt an impulse to grab the magnet back, but she couldn't make herself do it. "You've won Oz," she said. "You can have all the robes you want."

Mascara ran down Mumps' face in rivers. Some of it ran around her large trembling lips giving them a clownish black outline. She looked Sam briefly in the eyes and wailed, "It was marvelous."

But then the sorcessess noticed the magnet in her hand, and the way everyone was looking at her. She took a deep breath, and she stood up, and she held the Love Magnet out in front of her to show its power. Sam smiled. With this weapon, the Sorceress Lady Mumps was ready to lead the victory parade into the Emerald City, which surely would have fallen by now. She was ready take her place on the Emerald Throne.

The Sorceress Mumps collected her wits and went back to the window to resume her speech to the empty courtyard.

The Shaggy Man stooped down and reached below his shoe. He grabbed tightly the other magnet, which was squirming like a trapped animal. He held it out toward Mumps. And the Love Magnet flew out of her weak hand and sailed across the room and clapped with a metallic sound as the Shaggy Man caught it.

"Thought that might work," he said, and he held the two magnets together in his large hand.

"COME now," said Tik-Tok. "we HAVE A LONG walk to THE emerald CITY."

"What about the foxes and the elephants?" Thaddeus asked.

"All gone," said the Wogglebug looking down from the broken window.

Thirty-One

On the way to the Emerald City with their prisoners, the professor worked out what must have happened. "You remember the map we found in the tunnel?" he said. "It said, 'capital' beside the picture of the witch's castle. But I believe the foxes were told to undermine 'the capital,' meaning the Emerald City. But reading the word on the map where it was, they undermined the witch's castle in error. Foxes are sly but not very bright," he said.

No one could come up with a better explanation for the earthquake. And they all breathed easier in the hope that the true capital was unharmed.

And it was. Ozma was waiting for them when they arrived, having seen the earthquake in her magic picture—which had started working the moment the Wicked Witch was revived. She watched much but understood little of what she was seeing. After talking briefly to Tik-Tok and the Scarecrow, she ordered Mildred, Louise, and Thaddeus into a plush room in her palace, where there were games and books and padded furniture, as well as some very tasty bread and a few of the most prominent citizens of Oz to tell them stories and answer questions and keep them company.

Sam, Mumps, and Lloco-Monnem were locked away in separate rooms with plush chairs and tasty bread with sweet butter and storybooks richly illustrated. They all took advantage of the chairs, but only Mumps ate the bread. No one opened the storybooks.

The princess requested the presence of the Scarecrow, the Tin Woodman, the Cowardly Lion, the Patchwork Girl, Tik-Tok, Professor Wogglebug, and the Shaggy Man in her throne room. They sat around a table laden with good food, both cold and hot, and good drink, for those who partook of such things, and they told the princess all they had learned and all that had happened on their long adventure.

"My, my," said the princess, mostly satisfied. "But I must call in these children to fill in the missing pieces."

So she brought Mildred and Thaddeus and Louise to the table. The moment Louise saw Ozma, she felt as though she and the princess were old friends. She had read so many stories about her and had seen her picture so often that it took a moment to realize that even though she felt as though she knew Ozma well, Ozma did not know her at all. Louise wanted to run up to her and hug her. But Ozma looked at the group with such gravity that Louise knew she could not approach her unless she was asked to. The children were seated at the table and served even more delicious bread, plain and toasted, and eggs and fruit and oatmeal, and ice cream, and pie, and jam and all the hot chocolate and cider they could wish, and then, once they were well fed, Ozma asked each to tell the story of why they had come to Oz and what they wanted and how they had managed to get here and what they had done and who they were. And as they replied, she nodded much and asked more questions until she was satisfied that they had filled in all the gaps they could.

"Well, well," she said once everything was thoroughly talked out. "But there are still some things for me to know. Now it is time to talk to the others."

She brought the others in one at a time. Sam was first. When she was brought into the room Ozma was sitting on her throne. The Cowardly Lion crouched at her left and a very large tiger whom everyone but Sam knew was named The Hungry Tiger, crouched on her right. Sam was invited to sit at the table where she was given a plate of good food with pie and cider, which, despite being hungry, she ate very little of. And when she was ready, Ozma invited her to tell her story.

Sam put her elbows on the table. "I'm not afraid of you," she said.

Ozma smiled. "It's not my fault if after all this you still lack wisdom," the princess replied.

"Huh?"

Ozma left her throne and put down her tall staff and walked around the table. "We are almost ready to send home the children who are going home. The question I have to answer is whether you will be going with them. To answer that question, I will need to know a few things. I hope that is all right."

"What if I don't want to go home?"

"It's not a question of what you do or do not want," the princess said. "It's a question of what I decide."

Sam did not understand.

"Do you want to stay in Oz?" the princess asked.

"Why would she let her stay in Oz?" Mildred asked Louise in a whisper.

"I don't know. That's not like the books," Louise whispered back.

Ozma looked at Louise and Mildred sternly. They did not whisper again after that.

"That depends on what happens if I decide to stay," Sam asked.

"No, no, no," Ozma said with a smile while everyone else watched. "You don't understand. You cannot *decide* to stay. I can decide to make you stay or I can decide to send you back. I will decide that after you have told me your story. But the first question is what do you want? Do you hope to go home with…" and then she paused to think of the best words to use, "with your friends."

"With my…" but Sam understood better than to finish the thought she had begun. "What happens if you decide to let me stay?"

"That also depends on your story," she said. "I cannot say yet exactly what will happen. But I can tell you, you will get exactly what you deserve."

"You don't want someone like me in Oz," said Sam. "I'll go home."

"You mean you *want* to go home," said Ozma.

"What?"

"I see you are starting to understand. I don't have to send you home. I don't have to allow you to go home. You broke the laws of my country. Now I must decide what to do about that. I can send you home with your friends or I can keep you here for punishment. That is in my power, my authority, and my responsibility. Are you still not afraid of me?"

Sam looked at the stern yet somehow friendly face of the girl princess. Then she looked at the tiger on one side of her throne, licking its paw and rubbing its head, and the lion on the other side, yawning.

"If I don't do what you say, you'll use your animals on me," said Sam.

"Use them for what?" said Ozma. "We do not *use* animals in Oz. Tell me your story."

Sam realized at last that everything depended on her story. But it also depended on her telling the truth about her story. She did not know exactly how she knew this. But she was sure it was so. And that was a new and difficult position for her to be in. Under the gaze of the princess, however, she found she was able to tell the actual truth pretty well. She told her all that had happened from the moment in the playground to the moment she was then in, here at the table where ice cream was melting on her blueberry pie. And she made nothing up. She said nothing any of the other children could contradict. She even told how she tried to stomp on Louise's back, and how she told stories to Mister Farmer Simplit and Mistress Dairyma'am Plitsim so they would turn the other children away, and how she hoped to serve with the incomparable Lady Mumps. She wondered what her father would think of how she told the story.

"Thank you," said Ozma. And she ordered Sam a fresh plate of food.

"Then I can go home?"

"First, I will hear what the others tell me," said the princess without emotion.

The next to come was the Witch Lloco-Monnem who, with many a glance at the Hungry Tiger and the Cowardly Lion, told her a story of how she'd studied Oz for many years until she understood all about the dust of the witch and how she'd gone to Tin-Puh and how they'd followed the stories of the Lady Mumps and how they'd figured out a way to use her to take over this magical kingdom.

"But you know Oz would no longer be the wonderful place it is once you took it over," said Ozma.

"But it would be ours." Lloco-Monnem was as honest as Sam and did not apologize for anything. She told Ozma how she regretted the big mistake that caused the earthquake—but that was Tin-Puh's fault, she said. She admitted that she had lost and Ozma had won, and Ozma would do with her as she pleased.

Last, the princess summoned Lady Mumps. The sorceress was served a good meal at the table, which she ate rapidly as she spoke, and then asked for more. Ozma asked her to tell her story.

"It's not over," she said. "And you owe me a new robe."

Ozma just smiled. "But tell me your story," she said again, mildly.

"I am the Empress Sorceress Lady Mumps," she said. "That's my story. Do you have any more of this delicious cake?"

Ozma allowed her another piece of cake.

The princess realized quickly that Mumps did not understand very well what information Ozma was seeking or what position she was in. So she asked smaller questions: who are you? where do you come from? why are you here? But these questions did get not her very much farther. At one point Mumps pushed her empty plate in front of her and stood up as tall as her little legs would allow and announced, "I am Mumps. And you are all my subjects."

Without moving, the Hungry Tiger growled and Mumps burst

into a flood of tears and fell back into her chair, saying "please don't hurt me. It was all Tin-Puh's fault."

"What's happened to her?" Sam asked.

"Maybe you'd like to stay with her," Ozma replied.

Sam turned up her nose.

"What are you going to do with her?" asked Thaddeus.

"You could put her in prison," said Louise because she had read all the books.

"Oh, not right away. I think she'd feel too much at home there, so it would not work as a punishment, and that would not be kind," said Ozma.

"We now have a marvelous maze of tunnels," said the Wogglebug. "I think it may take many years for anyone put down in them to find their way out. We could send her down there. We could send all three of them down there."

Ozma went back to her throne and picked up her staff and sat.

"There is a room in the witch's castle full of elephants and foxes," she said. "They did not escape with the others because they are injured and lame from the hard work they did in clearing the land around the castle."

"Losers," Mumps bellowed. But no one seemed to hear.

Ozma continued without pause: "No one is caring for them. For the time being, it will be the job of these plotters to make them all healthy again. To nurse, to clean, to care for these lame elephants and lame foxes. This will give them and us time to think about what happens next."

"I want to go home," said Sam.

"Really?" Ozma asked.

"Please," said Sam.

"Perhaps I will send your friends home and send you back to your room where you can await my decision."

"Please," said Sam. "I want to go home."

Mildred stepped up to the throne and bowed. "Princess Ozma, please let her come with us."

"Does she not deserve the same punishment as the others?" the princess asked.

"She's just a kid," said Mildred. "And her mother will be worried."

Ozma looked at Mildred and smiled. Then she looked at Louise and Thaddeus.

"We go to a different school," said Louise.

Ozma called Louise and Thaddeus to stand with Mildred before her.

"As you wish. I am only sorry that I cannot get to know you brave children better. But I know you have people waiting anxiously for you, and I must get you back home."

"The Shaggy Man has the magnet," said Mildred.

"Ah, a little bit of a problem with that," said The Shaggy Man, holding up the two magnets, the four feet touching making the shape of a stretched circle. "Can't get them apart." He pulled hard. Then he handed the joined magnets to Ozma.

She turned it over in her hands. She said to Mildred, "How exactly did this magnet get you here?"

"We don't know," said Mildred.

"It probably wouldn't get you home anyway," she said. "If it was trying to get you here, then there must be an enchantment on it. It was waiting for its time. And when the time came, it chose you to carry it here. It won't want to take you back."

"Why would it want to bring Anti-Love to Oz?" Louise asked.

"Well, I won't know until I study this some more and consult those more familiar with these things than I am, but I wonder if it is that simple. I don't know if it came to Oz to join in the conquest or if it came to Oz to draw the Love Magnet where it needed to be to save us from…" and then she pointed, "from them."

"Wow," said Thaddeus. "So is it good or is it evil?"

"Well we don't know who enchanted it or why and we don't know the nature of the spell. We know only how it worked. But we do not know how it was meant. But don't worry. I have magic that will send you home."

"The magic belt," said Louise.

Ozma stood and hugged each of the children in turn. First Mildred, then Thaddeus, then Louise.

"Can I come back, someday?" Louise asked.

"Anything's possible," she said. "This is Oz." And then she looked over at Sam. "Come, join your friends, Samantha."

Sam stepped forward more slowly than she usually did.

"Good-bye," said the princess.

In a flash, the four of them were on the playground outside of Edgerton Elementary. They would never find out how they got there. School was in session. It was a cold day. Sam ran into the building to find her mother. Mildred and Thaddeus and Louise walked to Mildred's house. There was a police car in the driveway.

Thirty-Two

No one believed the children's story of course, although their tellings were remarkably similar. This led to all sorts of other stories about what *really* must have happened. The children were all questioned by the police, and doctors gave them all physicals, and Mildred's mother talked to all the parents about how children experience and respond to trauma and about the place of fantasy as a coping mechanism and the need to be patient and give them plenty of time. She told them what they should say and the best way to react, and it came down to not fighting with the children about what they all said happened. "The truth will come out someday, when they are ready." But for now they were all safe. No one had been injured.

There were only two consequences for Mildred. The first was that she was no longer allowed to walk home by herself after school, although sometimes when she knew her mother wouldn't be home, she still did. And the second was that when sides were chosen for kickball, Sam told Donny he had to put her on his team. Sam never let anyone complain about the quality of Mildred's play, no matter how often she made an out.

Interset Press is a small, independent press located in Southern New Hampshire. Lacking deep pockets for promotion in the crowded, competitive field of commercial fiction, it relies on word of mouth advertising. If you enjoyed this book, please tell your friends, rate the title on Amazon.com, or put a comment on our Facebook page.